LEO

ZODIAC KILLERS #9

WL KNIGHTLY

BRIXBAXTER PUBLISHING

Leo
Zodiac Killers #9

Copyright © 2018 by WL Knightly

All rights reserved. This book or any portion thereof may not be reproduced or used in any manner whatsoever without the express written permission of the publisher except for the use of brief quotations in a book review.
The novel is a work of fiction. Names, characters, places and plot are all either products of the author's imagination or used fictitiously. Any resemblance to actual events, locales, or persons – living or dead – is purely coincidental.

First Edition.

Editor: Eric Martinez
Cover Art: Kellie Dennis at Book Cover by Design

Find WL Knightly

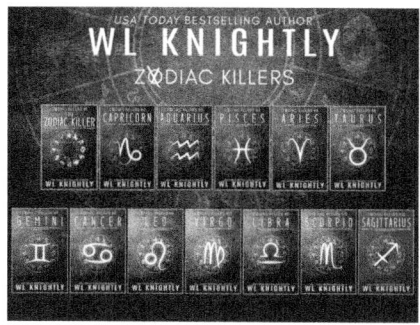

http://thezodiackillerseries.com

CHAPTER 1

CARTER

Carter stood at the window of his office looking out at the dimly lit parking lot where his secretary Peggy was getting into her car after a long evening of choir practice. A soft knock sounded at his door, and he closed the blinds and hurried to greet the visitor.

He had been expecting Keely Milton, a pretty little blonde who was new to his congregation and having a hard time dealing with a divorce that resulted from her having a miscarriage. He was hoping to offer her more than prayer to ease her troubles.

When he opened the door, he was pleased to see that Keely had dressed the part. Her low-cut dress was given a modest look with a white cardigan, but the heels she wore screamed harlot. He was about to find out which kind of girl she truly was.

"It's good to see you, Ms. Milton."

"Thank you for seeing me, Pastor Hamilton." She walked into the office and dropped her handbag in one chair as she sat in another across from his desk. "But please, call me Keely."

"Then I have to ask you to call me Carter." He gave a wink. "Pastor Hamilton reminds me so much of my father. Makes me realize how much I miss him." He gave a soft sigh, but in actuality, he had always had a rough relationship with his father who had wanted him to live up to his higher standards when Carter was much better at living up to his lower ones.

He was a chip off the old block when it came to one thing, and that was using his power as counselor and pastor to fuck the young women of the congregation.

"Of course. I'd rather call you Carter anyway." She gave him a warm smile as he walked over and sat on the desk in front of her.

He leaned forward and took her hand. "What can I do for you today, Keely?"

"I'm just having a hard time, I guess. I mean, I'm not sure if you've heard, but my husband and I split up recently after I miscarried our baby."

"Is that what happened, Keely?" He knew in his profession that the story others wanted him to hear wasn't often the truth. Keely had been so broken when she first arrived at the church, and she was trying too hard to pull off the good girl act. "God is telling me that he wants you to trust me, Keely. How might I endear myself to you so that you'll find me worthy of your confidence? Of your wicked truth?"

She shifted in her chair uncomfortably and brushed her fingers through her hair. "That's so amazing. How you knew, I mean." She wiped her eyes which had filled with tears so full they were about to spill down her cheeks. "There is more, but it's so hard."

"The truth will set you free. And what you confess here in the privacy of my office will not leave it. I'm sworn to keep confidence with everyone I counsel, the same way a doctor or lawyer is." He patted her hand, stroking it softly to comfort her.

More tears came, and he reached over and handed her a tissue. "Thank you," she said. "It's just I didn't want anyone here to know what I did. So, I lied about the miscarriage. I actually had an abortion. I bet you think I'm just horrible. My husband and I had already been having problems, and he had been messing around with a few other girls at the club I worked at."

"You were a waitress?"

She met his eyes but quickly looked away. "No, I—" She clammed up and pulled the hem of her dress down over her knees. "I was a dancer at a gentleman's club."

"Oh, I see." He patted her hand again and let it go, standing to his feet to walk to the window. He wanted her to feel a sting of disappointment, when in fact, it was the best news he'd heard all week.

"I'm sorry. It's so inappropriate. I know that now. I've changed. I'm trying to hard to do better. I just didn't want to lose my job; my body was all I had going for me, you know?"

"I understand. It had to be horrible seeing your husband want all of those other women, too."

She nodded as her face scrunched up into an ugly cry. "Yes, it was. He hadn't even been happy about the baby. And when he started messing around, I just wanted to put things back to how they were. I just wanted his attention again, but he was so angry. It was the final nail in the coffin of our troubled marriage."

"It's a shame."

"I know. I'm so ashamed." She put her head down and dabbed her nose and eyes.

He walked back over to the chair and knelt beside her. "No, that's not what I mean, dear one. You are letting him make you feel shame when he should have been cherishing you."

She lifted her head and looked into his eyes. "But I did a horrible thing."

He held on to the arm of the chair. "It is a horrible thing, yes, and I know God will give you the chance to atone for that sin. He's the only one who is allowed to judge you for it. Recognizing it is the first step. And you're already on your way to God's grace and forgiveness. You've confessed, admitted your sin. But I need you to do something for me, Keely. Something very important." He leaned in as if begging.

Keely nodded. "Yes, anything."

He reached out and touched her cheek. "I need you to stop beating yourself up. Forgive yourself. We're all sinners, Keely. Even I'm not perfect." He shook his head and pulled his hand away, closing his eyes. "Forgive me."

"For what? You've been so kind."

He looked back up with a pleading look. "It's just; you're so beautiful. I can't see how your husband would leave such a gorgeous woman like yourself."

"Thank you," she said, licking her lips and running her hand through her hair in a shy way as her cheeks flushed.

"Well, I'm a man. I recognize true beauty when I see it, and well, you know how we can be. Probably better than anyone else, having been in your profession."

She nodded. "I've seen how some men act, but you're a good man, Carter." She reached out and put her hand on his.

"Thank you. but God needs me to ask for your forgiveness."

"Oh, why? That's not necessary, Carter." She shook her head and gave him an apologetic look.

"I don't think we could continue until I do. It's just; I can't take my eyes off your body or stop myself from wondering what it would be like to kiss you and touch you. I mean, I don't want you to be uncomfortable. So please, forgive me." He shook his head and looked away again as if he were embarrassed.

She leaned forward. "Of course. Honestly, it's nice just to be noticed." She got a faraway look in her eyes. "I think it's what I miss most about my job. All of the attention."

"Well, you have mine." He chuckled. Then he stood up, and his erection was damned near eye level. He sat back on the corner of his desk and put his hand in front of it. "Forgive me."

She grinned. "It's not the first time I've given men that reaction." She gave a little giggle that made him want to bend her over his desk and bury himself deep inside her.

"Yes, but I don't want you to feel uncomfortable. My wife is a bit neglectful lately, and I'm only saying that because we're in confidence here."

"That's so sad. I heard she's away on the mission trip."

"Yes, she stays gone, and I try to behave, you know? Just trying to be a good husband." He hadn't been a good husband since he said the words "I do" and got a blow job in the men's room from one of his girlfriends a half hour after when it was time to change out of his tux.

"That's horrible. It must be lonely having her gone. I know how that is. I'm lonely too now. No one to talk to after a hard day and no one to snuggle with at night."

"Well, you can start coming to see me here, and we'll be lonely together. It's so refreshing when I find someone like yourself who I can confide with as well. It's always me listening, you know? But I know you'll keep what goes on behind these doors a secret."

"Oh, of course. Everything." She looked down at his crotch, and he got to his feet.

"I'm so sorry. The vulgar thing has a mind of its own. You must think I'm a degenerate." He started to step away, but she reached for his arm.

"No, I don't. It's no different than the men who used to come into the club. They just wanted a little attention is all."

"Did you give it to them?" He stopped himself and put his hand to his mouth. "I'm sorry. That was totally inappropriate."

She giggled. "I don't mind, Carter. I don't mind lots of things." She uncrossed her legs and then crossed them the other way as she bit her lip. "I mean, it's hard not to feel the same kind of feelings when I see how much of a reaction you have to me. I like being adored."

"You're just so beautiful. I can't help it. You're a little temptress. God is telling me that it is one of your gifts. In a sense, you bring healing to men with your body. It's just not acceptable to most, but he just gave me a word that it is not your fault. He made you this way, He said. You shouldn't be judged, but it's the world who puts the blame on us and tries to steal our light. You should let yours shine, Keely. Let it shine brightly."

"Really?" She moved to the edge of her seat. "That's all I've ever wanted to do is make others feel happy."

"And I'm sure you've made a lot of men very happy." He smiled big and then got up to walk around to his chair behind the desk.

"I have. I could show you how. If God would be okay with it?" Her eyes burned on his.

She was finally playing his game. "I know it's wrong, but if it would make you feel better? I mean, we could do this as a form of therapy."

"How?" She surely seemed interested and eager.

"Well, in order to help you, I'm afraid I'm going to need you to tell me all of the dirty things you've done and ask for forgiveness. You might even have to demonstrate a few of them."

"Could I do that now?"

"I think so. I mean, it might be better if the door was locked." He smiled at her, and when she got to her feet, she walked over and locked the door.

Then she walked around the desk and got to her knees. "Some of the men, they'd whisper in my ear and ask me to blow them for a little extra money."

"And did you do that?" He was turned on by her telling him the confessions and hoped she had a lot of them.

"I needed the money. It's how I met my husband."

"Dirty girl. He knew what he was getting into then from the start."

"Yeah, I suppose he did." She looked at his bulge and looked up into his eyes as she reached over and rubbed it.

"Then it's not your fault. He knew what was important to you when you met."

She nodded and undid his pants. "Yes, he did."

"I have a feeling that you try really hard to be a good girl, don't you, Keely?"

She nodded. "I've tried so hard lately." She took a deep breath. "But it's like I don't fit in here, you know? Some of the other ladies are so judgmental. You're not, though."

"Because I'm ordained by God. His word falls directly in my ears like someone whispering divine secrets to a chosen friend. You did the right thing coming to me."

She slowly reached into his pants and rubbed the length of his cock, which was hard and ready for her. "I have another confession."

"Confess your little heart out, sweetheart. I'm here to listen. Here for you to do anything you want or need to do to help you."

"I've watched you on the stage. Seen how powerful and admired you are. I've thought of what it would be like to fuck you." She covered her mouth. "I'm sorry. I know cursing is bad."

"It's our secret too, Keely. I'm sure we'll have many of them." His cock was weeping, it was so ready for her mouth, and when she leaned forward and closed her lips around it, he stared down at her and ran his fingers through her hair.

"That's a good girl." He stroked her hair as she worked him, taking him balls deep until she nearly gagged. He loved the professionals and could usually spot one in a heartbeat.

As he sat there, getting some of the best head of his life, a knock sounded at the door.

"Fuck," he said quietly. He pulled her away, and she wiped her mouth, hurried around to the chair, buried her face in a tissue, and began to fake sobs as he walked to the door.

He opened it and found Ava Lindsey standing there with her hand on her hip. "Why is the door locked?" she asked, peeking around him.

"I'm in a counseling session, Ava. May I help you?"

"We had an appointment tonight too, or did you forget?" She gave him a cold stare. He hadn't expected this little tryst to go on so long.

"I'm sorry." He stepped out into the hall and shut the door behind him. "Come to the house later; I'll make it up to you."

She shook her head. "And what's going on with the girl in your office? I've seen her in church, and some of the women aren't happy at the way their husbands look at her."

"She's suffering after a miscarriage and a divorce. She's seeking counsel and nothing more. The poor creature knows that you all hate her, by the way."

"Because she's a slut. And don't think I don't see what's going on."

Carter had not wanted to fight with her. Not when he had that mouth waiting for him on the other side of the door. "Are you done?"

She let out a long sigh. "I'll be over later. Leave the back door open so I can slip in."

"Fine. See you then." He leaned over and kissed her, and she pulled away, shook her head, and then hurried out.

"I'm sorry, Keely," he said as he walked back into the room. "Where were we?" He shut the door and locked it.

As he walked over, she got up and leaned against his desk. "Do you think God would forgive me for this?" She spread her legs, showing off her soft pink gash, then tossed him her panties, which he caught and brought to his nose.

He walked over, and she hurried to free his cock as he brought his mouth down on hers for a quick kiss. He couldn't wait to get inside of her. "You're already forgiven, angel."

CHAPTER 2

DAREK

Darek sped across town with Lizzy in the seat beside him, and he felt like his day was never going to end. It started off horribly, having to go and see that idiot, Ken Sin. He and Lizzy had agreed to make him suffer the consequences of his false confession in order to keep the case from imploding while they waited for the real killer to make another move. What they hadn't planned was the asshole going crazy over their headfuck and smashing Lizzy face-first into a table.

Luckily, nothing had been broken, but she looked like she'd done twelve rounds with Tyson. To make things worse, before Darek could even leave the hospital, he found out Justin was dead, and they'd gotten a call in from work. His brothers in blue reported a body that had been found inside an abandoned warehouse, and the description fit Mia.

Total nightmare day, and it wasn't over yet.

He couldn't stop thinking about Justin. Taken out by a home invasion? It was all too much. Despite the fact that the remaining members of the Zodiac Society were supposed to be banding together for survival, two more had died since the meeting in New Orleans, and with each and every passing, the killer got closer to Darek. So far, the others had all died in the order their signs were on the Zodiac, starting with Capricorn. Darek was certain this was more than a coincidence, and it hadn't escaped his attention that he could possibly be the last man standing.

With the driver confessing that the shooting in New Orleans was a hit, he'd have to questions all of the remaining Zodiacs to see who had enemies. Since Justin had gotten gunned down in his home, Darek had to believe that it could have possibly been him with the target on his back.

"You're quiet," said Lizzy, who had been quiet too. "What are you thinking?"

Darek pulled up at the scene and stopped the car. He looked at her. The flashing lights reflecting off her bruised face didn't detract from her beauty one bit. "I'm just tired."

"It's been a hell of a day." She opened the opened the door and got out, and he followed, meeting her in front of the car as she walked into the crowd of officers and onlookers.

Darek saw the blood as they approached and realized his clothes were still covered in Lizzy's. Thank God it was dry, but he had to stop her. "Hey, hang back. We don't want to contaminate anything with your blood."

"Shit," she said as if she had forgotten. "I should have gone home first."

"Let's see if we've got a positive ID, and let forensics be your hands."

"Good plan." She rolled her eyes, and he noticed that the others were all staring at her. "Looks like I'll be the talk around the water cooler in the morning."

"Max should be here by now." As much as Darek wanted to kill the guy for making moves on Lizzy, he knew he had to be on his best behavior. He and Lizzy had both made mistakes, and a hot temper wasn't going to help anything, especially when Max might have to identify Mia's dead body. He hoped it wasn't her. He didn't want to have to call Bay Collins with that kind of news.

Lizzy walked up to Darius. "Have you seen Max?"

"No, not yet. It took us a minute to track him down, but he's on his way." The man shook his head and looked over at the body where the forensics team was busy taking photographs. "I called you as soon as I saw her. She's been stabbed more than a few times. Reminded me of the Zodiac's victims."

"Jesus," she said.

"I'll do the ID," said Darek.

"I just thought he could get here quicker; I wonder what he's up to that he couldn't beat us here. This is his part of town."

Darek was bitter knowing how she knew that and wondered how much time they'd actually spent together. "Yeah. I got this." He walked over and looked down at the girl. Her face was partially covered by her hair, and while she was very similar to Mia in shape, size, and age, her nose was not the same, and she had a tattoo of a star just under her earlobe. Bay would never let Mia have such a thing.

"It's not her." He stepped away from the body. "I'm positive." It made him sick the things that people could do to each other, and his nerves were on edge with the victim's wounds looking a hell of a lot like the Zodiac's victims. He grabbed the sleeve of one of the forensics team. "We'll need to have Cobb check out the wounds and go over her with a fine-toothed comb. I want to know if there is any relation between this girl and the other victims."

The man nodded as Darek stepped away to see Lizzy. "Well, at least Max and Bay will be happy."

About that time, a familiar voice got Darek's attention.

"Move the fuck out of the way!" shouted Bay as he pushed past one of the onlookers. "Why didn't you call me!" He raked his hand through his hair.

Darek realized he must have been listening to the dispatcher's radio. "It's not her. It's not Mia."

"Are you sure?"

Max walked up next, acting cool as a cucumber. "Where have you been?" asked Darek.

"Around," Max said with a shrug. "Darius said you needed me?"

Darek noticed Bay's eyes widen, and he knew to make it clear he hadn't called Max there when he hadn't informed Bay. "Lizzy wanted you to come and check it out."

"You should have called me," said Bay. "I've been worried sick." He turned to Max, his temper flared and his eyes wild. "That could have been her! And if anything ends up happening to her, I'm coming for you, motherfucker."

"So charming." Max nudged Darek. "You see why she bailed on him. He's an obsessive asshole. Probably killed her himself."

Darek couldn't help but notice that Max wasn't broken up over the idea, nor was he upset or worried over Mia. He pulled Bay away and spoke quietly. "Go home, Bay. This isn't Mia; you got the information you came for. Now go home, and if she turns up, dead or alive, you have my vow that you'll be the first person I call." He walked Bay through the crowd, leaving Max and Lizzy with the body.

When they got to his car, which was sitting with the door wide open, the keys still inside. Bay took a deep breath. "Do you think it was the killer?"

"I don't know. It could be. But look, I walked you out here to tell you something. I went to call Justin about the hit theory, and when I did, Brandy told me some terrible news."

Bay's eyes narrowed as Darek tried to find the right way to tell him. He looked over his shoulder to make sure no one else had walked up on them. Then he met Bay's eyes. "Justin's dead."

"What? How is that even possible?"

"Brandy said he was gunned down in his home." Darek knew that didn't make a lot of sense, and the randomness was just too unbelievable.

"Holy fuck. Who was it? Do you think it was the killer?"

"I don't know. With Justin dead, there aren't many of us left." The thought scared Darek. "Carter, Lane, and Ethan have to be notified. I want them to take every precaution they can. We lost Corey and Justin since the meeting, and with the shooting happening so soon before he was gunned down at home, I'm wondering if he could have been the reason for the hired hit. Surely, he had some enemies."

Bay shook his head, and Darek wondered if it even bothered him at all. "It makes sense if his death was a random home invasion, which I hardly think is the case. What about that Betty person? He had no idea who that was. She could be anyone."

"Look, we'll talk about it, okay? I'll call you in the morning, and hopefully by then, I'll know if this case has Zodiac written all over it. So far, it's not looking good for that line I'm walking. It's growing thinner by the minute. I just need you to stay at home and try to calm down."

Bay got in his car and started it up. Then he looked up at Darek, who stood by his open door. "I'll calm down when she's safe." He let out a breath. "I've never felt so much at once when I thought that could be her."

Darek doubted he'd ever felt much of anything but anger and annoyance and was surprised that he'd admitted it to him. The two had become reluctant friends. "I know, man. Get home and get some rest. I've got to get back to the investigation."

He turned and walked away as Bay shut his car door, and he looked into the crowd of onlookers to see if anyone looked like they might be capable of committing a crime like this. The old adage about the murderer returning to the scene wasn't always true, but many times, it was.

Lizzy waved him over, and he took a deep breath and joined her. "Did they find anything?"

"Not yet. I wanted you to see this." She pointed down to the girl's wrist where another tattoo was.

"What's that say?" He couldn't quite make out the font, and with the amount of blood coating her wrists and arms, it was hard to tell if that was the entire tattoo.

She crossed her arms. "I think it says Antonio, so let's hope that's her boyfriend and a possible suspect."

"Hey," said Max as he nudged Darek. "If you don't need me, I'm heading out."

Darek couldn't believe what he was hearing. "What's with you, man? You used to live for shit like this. Now you're late to show, and you're the first to leave?" Darek also wanted to mention that he had not wasted any time moving in on his girl but didn't think he needed to make his day any more complicated.

"Sorry, I'm just not feeling it." Max looked out over the crowd, not meeting his eyes. "Besides, I have company at home. I want to get back before she bails, and you two have it under control." He started to walk away, and Darek followed.

"It's not Mia, is it?" Darek wouldn't put it past him to know exactly where she was.

Max narrowed his eyes at Darek. "Come on, man. You really think I'd keep that from you?"

"I don't know, man. I don't think we're as close as we used to be, and you didn't seem to wonder for a moment if this girl was Mia. Didn't you care about her?"

"It didn't cross my mind that it could be her. I've honestly gotten over her. I mean, I hope she's okay, but she dumped me. I'm not one to sit around pouting. You know how it is. You moved on pretty fast from Lizzy."

Darek couldn't believe he was going to go there. "Yeah, funny you should mention that. It's yet another reason I wouldn't put anything past you."

Max smiled. "I guess she told you. Hey, you can't blame me for that. She's the one who came on to me." He held his hands up. "Talk to her, man."

As he walked away, Darek wasn't sure if he knew the man anymore. Funny how things changed.

CHAPTER 3

CARTER

As Carter walked through the fellowship hall of his church on his way to his office, he wondered if someone had turned on the heating unit by mistake. The air felt thick like a blanket, and he was nearly about to perspire by the time he crossed the large auditorium and found his way to the front of the building where Peggy sat behind a large window at her desk.

The older woman, who was now probably in her early fifties, had been his father's mistress years ago and had been a faithful employee of the church for nearly twenty years. And while she was at one time a very attractive woman, the years of keeping secrets had taken its toll on her physically. She had permanent lines from the scowling expressions she reserved for Carter since his father's death, which was when he stepped up to the pulpit to take over. The other fine lines and wrinkles were from not knowing whether Carter would keep his word and keep her employed or if he'd find a way to throw her out on her ass.

As if. She didn't know it, but he'd promised his old man on his deathbed that he would take care of Peggy, and more than that, she knew too much. The only way to get rid of her was to kill her, and he had a feeling old Peggy would just come back to haunt him, or worse, be waiting in Hell for him when his time came to bust its gates wide open.

"What's the thermostat set on?" he asked. "It's so hot we'd make the devil feel right at home."

"It's the air conditioning," said Peggy. "I tried to call you earlier, but you didn't answer your phone."

He tried to avoid Peggy like the plague, and she knew it. She also knew his preference. "You could have texted me. I've told you a million times if I don't answer, it's the best way to get in touch."

"I've got a new phone, and I haven't figure out how to work it yet."

"Not my problem, Peg. Have Eddie come to see me." He walked into his office and shut the door, certain that Peggy was cursing under her breath. He had hated her since he was a boy, running up and down the church pews and playing in the baptismal.

He smiled looking at the mess he'd left his desk in, and while he tidied it up, he thought about power-fucking Keely and how hot it had been when she'd taken it hard and dirty. He had truly found the perfect little broken angel for his amusement.

Ava hadn't found it amusing at all that he had been in the meeting so late and let him know about it when she showed up for their rendezvous. He had hoped to blow her off now that her entitlement was getting out of control, and she was becoming less and less easy to manipulate. He needed his women malleable, easy to control and ready to conform to his needs and desires, all while being completely discreet.

Ava had gotten sloppy lately. Showing up to his office when she felt like it and making accusations that, while they were true, were certainly none of her concern. He had told her from the start it would never be more than just a little fun.

He finished straightening up and tossed a few things into the trash. Then a knock sounded on his door. "Come in," he called, knowing the familiar knock was Eddie Landon.

Sure enough, a moment later, the older man walked into the room. He had been Carter's father's right-hand man and had been like an uncle to Carter since the day he was born. "Hey, Peg said you were here. I was going to come and talk to you about the air unit. It's been giving us problems, and well, I didn't want to say anything to Peggy, but it damned near burned the place down this morning. I found it smoking, and it seems the main power board in it is fried."

"Have it replaced. It should be under warranty, right? We just put the damned thing in five years ago." He had built the new Church, which was supposed to be state of the art, but apparently, they had gotten a bum air unit.

Eddie raked his hand through his salt and pepper hair. "It's not under warranty. The building is nearly six years old, and we only had a five-year warranty. Hopefully, I found it in time, and they can just replace the circuit board, but if not and the unit is fried, it's going to cost quite a bit for a new one. Money we can't afford to spend right now."

"We couldn't fall back on one of the others?" There were other units in the church. If all else failed, maybe they could use the board from one of those.

"No, each unit is specific to its building, and the one that's out was already pushing it to feed that large of an auditorium. None of the others are big enough."

"So, we'll buy another unit."

"With what?"

"We don't even know if there is a problem, Eddie. You're worrying for nothing. Besides, I'll just preach about giving. Throw a little guilt on the flock, and they'll cough it up."

"You might want to rethink that. Most of our congregation are hurting right now. Besides, your father never preached about giving when he'd just gotten a new car. It looks bad."

"The car was voted in as part of my salary," said Carter. "It was their idea."

"I'm aware, and while many of the elders and deacons believe you are more than deserving, there are those who believe that you are spending the church's money a bit too frivolously. The television costs, the dues on the private jet, the trips you've been taking. This last one was spur of the moment and unplanned. Some of them are hearing complaints, and it's making them ask me questions. Something has to give, and I'm afraid it will be you."

Carter's temper flared. How dare they question him? He had always put the church first. "I'm their star. They can't get rid of me. So what that I took a personal trip? Surely the men can understand that I have a right to go and see an old friend. And I did work while I was in New Orleans. I even stayed a few extra days to make sure that I counseled one of our former members." He had also spent a lot of time checking on his friends. The shooting had come out of nowhere, and he had never been so glad to miss a free meal. He might have been killed. Perhaps it was divine intervention or just pure dumb luck.

Eddie gave him a pleading look. "I'm just saying, you need to slow down. I don't want everything you've worked for to implode. Kingdoms fall a lot harder and faster than they are built."

Carter recognized the words were his father's, but he couldn't imagine all that he'd built being taken away by a simple air unit. "We have millions."

"Our money is tied up with production and airtime since we've gone televised, and we're millions in debt. You depleted everything for the down payment and fees of building this church, and while we have some money coming in, many of our top guarantors have left the congregation because you can't keep your dick in your pants. We've spent thousands in hush money to keep you from getting sued."

Carter had had a few fallings out with several of the men in the church over the past year, but he hadn't been worried about it making too much of an impact. It was the hush money he knew would come back to bite him. But those women were mostly liars. "Okay, I get it. Just get someone out, and let's see what we're dealing with." He wasn't even sure what kind of money he was talking about. He wouldn't stress over anything until he knew what was going on, and even then, he'd let someone else stress for him. "We'll have to prepare Todd for tomorrow's sermon. I want him in the pulpit again."

Eddie shook his head and gave him a sideward look. "That's three Sundays in a row, Carter. You need to preach this Sunday. That's another thing everyone notices, you know? You're not earning your salary if you're not preaching."

"Oh yeah? And have they noticed that I'm the one who made this church what it is?"

"With their money, and it's that kind of attitude that's going to make them replace you."

Carter laughed it off. "They can't do that. This is my father's church, my church, and I'm going to remain the pastor here. None of them will replace me. I'm adored by the elderly here, the ones who watched me grow up and their children? They were all my friends and classmates. They loved me. Besides, Todd is an okay stand-in, but he's not got what it takes to make this place what it is."

Eddie shook his head. "The elderly who adored your father have all died, Carter, and their children, the ones you went to school with, they are all moving farther and farther away from the church. You'll be lucky to have a handful of your classmates left in the community by the end of the year. The new people? Most are single women, all drawn in by your good looks. They don't make any money, much less tithe."

"Get us someone here to look at the unit, and I'll preach next Sunday. Besides, Todd's on a roll."

Eddie opened the door. "They come for your word, not his. But that could change if you let him keep talking. And will you please at least be in attendance? I'm not sure I can keep covering for your ass."

Carter hadn't planned on being in attendance but decided it was the least he could do. With his wife out of town, he had been doing the Wednesday Bible studies so he could see Keely. "Fine. I will be there." He waved his hands to shoo Eddie away. "I'll prepare a special prayer for our air unit, but I need us up and running for tomorrow."

Eddie let out a long breath. "I'll see what I can do, but maybe it's time you start praying for a miracle. If it's this hot tomorrow, we'll have to call it off or move the service."

Carter made a sound of frustration. They had never canceled service, and if they had to, he would surely lose a lot of money in the process. "Let's hope it doesn't come to that."

"If it does, you can bet that the brethren won't be happy. I'll have to do a lot of damage control." He stepped out the door and closed it behind him.

"That's what you're good at, Eddie," he said, loud enough for the man to hear him through the door. He pulled out his phone and saw that his wife had called. Ignoring it, he went to the voice recorder on his device and took out his tablet. It was time to write a prayer that would have everyone digging into their pockets.

CHAPTER 4

DAREK

Monday morning, Darek was surprised that Max had come in and hurried out with Darius. He didn't mind being avoided, but while it was for the best, it wasn't like Max. He had yet to confront Lizzy again, not wanting to ask too many questions, but her messing around with his friend bothered him on a level he hadn't expected.

As he sat at his desk quietly working on the case notes from the most recent body dump, Lizzy took notice that something was wrong and confronted him.

"Are we going to talk about it?" she asked, leaning on the corner of his desk.

He shrugged, not wanting her to know just how much it had upset him. He really had no room to be upset, with Raven having been in the picture, but he couldn't help the way he felt. And if the whole "she came onto him" thing was true, then that just made it all worse. "Talk about what?"

She held up her hands defensively. "Okay, if that's how you want to play it, but know this. If you don't talk about it now, then I don't want to talk about it later."

The office was empty, and he realized that she was right. It was better just to get it all out in the open and behind them. They had too many obstacles as it was, most she didn't even know about, and he needed to seize the day and make the most of everything. If he had learned one thing by losing the other Zodiacs, it was that time was a precious thing. "I just don't want us to have problems. Life's too short, you know?"

"And that's why I think we should talk about it and put it behind us, but hey if you don't want—"

"Did you make the first move?" That was the only part he needed to be clarified.

"It wasn't a deliberate strategized event. It just happened, but yes, if you must know. I kissed him first." She crossed her arms. "You had found it so easy to move on, I guess I just wanted to see if it was possible for me, but I quickly learned that it wasn't. Max took it as an invitation to more, and I said that I wasn't ready. *I* wasn't." The *you were* hung silently in the air between them.

Darek got up to go and pour himself another cup of coffee, not really sure how to react, but Lizzy followed, knowing she wasn't going to let him clam up again.

She rose from her place on his desk and joined him. "As I said, it was nothing, Darek. Nothing at all. I somehow don't think that you could say the same about your friend."

Darek didn't open his mouth. He knew Raven had been about more. "That was all I wanted to know, okay? I can see how things happen, things we don't expect. We put ourselves in a position, and things just happen sometimes, but it's behind us."

Lizzy reached up and put her arms around his neck. "I agree. Let's leave it there."

The two of them being alone in the room was a rare thing, and Darek was fully prepared to make the most of it. He leaned in and brought his lips down on hers. As their kiss deepened, nothing else in the world mattered.

Suddenly, Reed's voice carried across the front office, giving Lizzy and Darek little time to break their lip lock at the coffee bar. "I want to know if that fool had anything to do with it," he called back to the chief as the two went their separate directions and he entered the room.

Reed hadn't seen Lizzy's injured face, and she was a bit nervous about what his reaction would be. She gave Darek a hesitant look and then turned around slowly to greet the man who was like an uncle to her.

Darek watched as Reed's face went white. "That animal did this?" he asked. Darek had told him what happened, but he must not have realized how bad it would look.

Lizzy brushed it off, still wiping her lips from the kiss. "It's not as bad as it looks."

"That bastard. I hope he gets his ass beat again in there. But in the meantime, I want you," he turned to Darek, "to get me some information on his religious affiliations. Find out if he's spoken to any member of the clergy, what church he used to attend, and if any of them have ever heard him talk about cults. This maniac didn't just wake up one day with this idea. A seed like this is planted and tended, nurtured. He's learned his tricks from someone, probably the best. The DA is actually starting to believe his story, and I want you to dig deeper." He seemed as if he were shutting Lizzy out.

"Hey, are you talking to him or both of us? I'm right here." She didn't like being left out, and Darek knew that Reed was going to have a hard time putting her back out there where Ken Sin was concerned.

"I think you need a few days off. I heard about that stunt you pulled. The goading. You riled him up."

"I riled him up," said Darek. The look on Reed's face told him the man wasn't buying the story. "Okay, we both did. It was the only way to keep him. We didn't want the case to fall stale, and we were hoping that if we kept him, we could sit and wait for the real killer to make a move. The man was making us look like fools."

"Well, he's bought himself some time with a real crime now," said Reed. He put his hand on Lizzy's shoulder. "He won't get away with this. But I meant what I said. Go home, get comfortable for a few days. Rest your mind and heal. Let's see what your partner here is made of." He turned back to Darek, and he nodded, ready for the challenge.

He suddenly felt like a string of luck might come his way, and he knew just the preacher to call in about Ken Sin. But then Reed's words planted a seed in his own mind. What if Ken Sin had been nurtured? What if the person who planted the seed was the real killer hoping to deflect attention away from himself or to have someone do the dirty work for him? Carter Hamilton could have done just that. It was a longshot, he knew, but still, an interesting theory. Bringing Carter in would surely force him to reveal if his relationship with Ken Sin was more than he'd made it out to be.

Having Carter come and talk to Ken would surely help Darek get a leg up for his promotion. He had to do all he could to appease Reed, and with Lizzy sitting out a few days, he and Carter could talk more about what happened. He could feel him out.

He still had to figure out who the hit was put on, and while Justin seemed the most likely candidate, having been gunned down, he wanted to make damned sure no one else had a target on their back, or worse, had one on everyone else's. With Carter staying behind after he'd said he was leaving, there was a good possibility it could have been to make sure the hit was carried out. Maybe he felt things were closing in. He could have wanted the Zodiacs out of the world completely so he would never be found out.

Darek looked Reed right in the eye. "I'll get right on it, sir."

"Excuse me," Lizzy said, pulling Sam aside. "I'm not one to sit down on the job. I want to get back on my horse when I fall down, and you know it."

"I also know you've been working hard and you need to take a day and make sure your head is on straight."

"But we have a new victim, and we're waiting on Cobb to tell us if this could be a part of our Zodiac case."

"You're talking about the girl who was found? The night you got your face slammed into a table?" He turned and gave Darek an accusing look. "You should have taken her home and checked out the scene yourself."

Darek felt the need to defend Reed's logic. "With all due respect, you and I both know Lizzy wouldn't have gone home."

Reed's jaw tightened, the muscles twitching slightly. "Next time, call me. I'll make sure she listens."

Darek wasn't going to argue with him, but there would be no way she'd have let that happen. "Yes, sir." He looked over at Lizzy, who shook her head.

Lizzy was swelled up with anger. "I don't want to take a day. Cobb will be calling soon, and I'll need to go down and make sure this doesn't link up with our case. Besides, the DA should be fucking happy about what we accomplished." Lizzy's voice was tinged with desperation and anger.

"Fuck the DA! You can call Dr. Cobb from the comfort of your couch for all I care, but you're sitting out. That's an order!" His temper was flared and his voice loud.

Lizzy grabbed her handbag and briefcase from under the desk and then shut off her computer. Without a word, she stormed out of the office.

"She's not going to be happy," said Darek, knowing that a break was only going to irritate her more than working would.

"I don't care. It's my call, and she should take a goddamned day. Robert would roll in his grave if he saw her face beaten like that. And I promised him I'd look after her. This is the only power I have over her, and one fucking day won't kill her." He turned, and after making a sound of frustration, he headed for the door. Once he got there, he looked back over his shoulder. "Make sure you don't waste any time. Let's get anything we can on this asshole."

Darek waited until he was gone and then hurried out after Lizzy, who was driving away. At least Reed had provided a little time and an excuse to do a little digging on his own without Lizzy over his shoulder.

CHAPTER 5

CARTER

Carter pulled into his private parking space Monday morning, knowing he was about to do a walk of shame of epic proportions. Not only had he missed another sermon, but he had made himself totally unreachable.

While he had no excuse for missing another Sunday service, he had prepared to tell the others that he had been in a long prayer session with the Lord and that he could not be disturbed. *Who would argue with that?*

"Where the hell were you yesterday?" asked Peggy as soon as he walked through the door. "I tried to reach you all day. We nearly sent out a search party, but someone saw your car at home."

Leave it to Peggy. He started across the fellowship hall and into the auditorium as the woman stayed on his heels with a pastry in one hand and her Starbucks in the other. "I can't help when the Lord wants to speak to me. And when that happens, it's not like I can just turn him off and put him out of my head. You have no idea how hard it is to have the big man upstairs for a boss."

She looked him dead in the eyes. "I'd imagine it's easier than trying to shovel that load of bullshit at me and making me believe it."

The woman had gone crass in her older years, and while Carter knew better than to try and fool her with his excuses, he sure hoped that they would hold water with the rest of the brethren.

He stopped to pull out his keys and unlock the door since her hands were too full to use her own key. "I'll be in my office." He walked past her desk and through the connecting door which he promptly locked behind him. He walked over to the door that led to the main hall, which he liked to leave open so that he could look out and see everyone coming his way.

Before he could get good and settled back in his seat, Eddie walked into his office. "Hey, Carter."

"Good morning, Eddie. You're here early." He hadn't expected to see him so soon but had a feeling it had to do with the fact that the church didn't feel like the depths of hell. "You got the air fixed I see. Just in time for Sunday service I presume."

"Yeah, and you're not going to like the bill when you see it. Rush jobs on weekends cost a hell of a lot more than scheduled ones during the work week." He walked over and moved a chair back to get around it and then sat across from Carter. He reached into his pocket and handed Carter a slip of paper he'd folded into a nice tight rectangle.

Carter unfolded it and read the damage. "This is nearly thirty grand!"

"Yeah, as it turns out, you needed more than one air handling unit for that large of an area. They worked into the night trying to get us ready for the Sunday service, and we would have lost more than that if they had needed to close us down."

"I guess we're lucky that's all it was." Carter shrugged and passed the bill across to Eddie, who could barely meet his eyes.

"Well," he said. "That's not all it cost unfortunately." He folded the paper and put it back in his pocket.

Carter eased back in his chair. "What now?"

"I'm afraid the brethren voted to stop paying for the private jet dues. They think it's impractical and said if you wanted one, you could buy it yourself."

"Clearly, they think I have a lot more money than I do." Carter was well off, but owning a jet outright was much more expensive than co-leasing with others.

"They know what you're bringing home, which is well above what they think you're worth at the moment."

"What's that mean?"

"It means if you miss another Sunday, they just might hand your reins over to Todd."

"I was lost in deep prayer—"

Eddie held up his hand. "Save that bullshit for the brethren. I'm not buying it. It's harder and harder to defend you, Carter. You're getting worse than your old man, and that's saying a lot. I never thought anyone could be worse than him. I told you not to miss again."

"Fine, I'll make sure not to miss again. It's just hard staying in the same damned routine month after month and year after year. When we're not filming, I like to have a little break. And now you're taking away the private jet, it's not like I'll have any desire to fly anywhere."

"I think that was the point. The elders and deacons thought that this might be the best way to clip your wings. You keep it up, and they'll make you sell the car."

"Noted," said Carter. His temper was flared, and he felt like a scolded child. "I still think they need to be reminded who the money maker is around here. And now I'm just going to cost them more airfare when I'm invited to speak."

"You've been getting fewer and fewer invitations, Carter. I'm telling you, they are doing their homework, and they are tired of your antics. Heed my advice. I never steered your father wrong." Eddie got to his feet and walked to the door. "I'll be down the hall if you need me."

His phone rang, and while he didn't feel much like talking to anyone, he noticed that it was Ava. She hadn't called that early in ages. She had grown much bolder though, and he was going to have to put a stop to it. He answered the phone and kicked back with his feet up. "Hello, Ava."

"Carter, hey." He could hear the sound of covers shuffling and her bed letting out a squeak. He imagined her in her bed still, lying between the satin sheets with nothing on but a smile.

"It's early, you know? I might have still been at home with Adrian."

"Yeah, but I know she's still on her little mission trip, and since you missed the service yesterday, I imagined you'd want to go in early and do some damage control."

"You do know me like a book." Which was part of the problem. Ava had learned too much about him and his habits.

"Well since your wife is gone, we should make use of the time. It's not often I get to be with you this early in the morning." She gave a little giggle.

He hadn't allowed her to stay the night because he didn't want her getting too comfortable. *Too late.*

"I had hoped we could meet for lunch today. There's a lot I need to talk to you about."

"It's not a good idea. Every elder and deacon of my church is out to get me, and I have to be on my best behavior."

Ava let out a sound of frustration. "Sneaking is all the fun. You've said so yourself."

"Yes, it usually is."

"Then come on, meet me for lunch," she said. "You won't be sorry, and I'll give you something special for dessert." The offer was quite enticing as he did like fucking Ava. But he thought his time would be better divided between playing up to the church staff and making a good impression.

"Please," she added. "I'll make it worth your while."

"Fine, I'll meet you. But just for an hour. I need to get back and try and behave."

He looked at his watch. He had a few hours to kill before lunch and decided to make the most of it. "I'll see you then," he said.

"Soon, baby," she said, ending the call.

Ava had been a fixture in his life for some time, and when the two had first started messing around, it was much the same as all the others. They had been content to sneak touches and share small secret glances across the crowd. The thrill of them having a secret together made their encounters intense, especially when his wife was around.

In fact, it had gotten to a degree where he was thinking of her so much, he had totally put his feelings for his wife aside, and while he didn't care much for Adrian after their I dos, it was a dangerous game to play. One that could end in divorce and dent his bank account.

He had quickly recognized the slip and corrected it, but they still continued to sneak around, their relationship redefined by their intent which was solely to get each other off.

But despite all of his efforts, the woman had still become so familiar with him, she knew him better than Adrian.

She was becoming a problem, but there was only one way to get rid of problems, and he knew better than to think he could afford to pay her off to get rid of her.

He needed to collect on a few of his loans, and he pulled out his phone to see who owed him what. There were a few friends listed, some owing no more than a hundred here or there, and one name that stuck out more than the rest. "Justin Finch." He dialed the number, and while it rang, he thought of how the man had contacted him about his friend's situation. The girl had been engaged to Corey, about to start a new life together when he'd passed away. So, when Justin called him needing him to sign a fake marriage certificate and say that he'd been the one to marry the couple in New Orleans, Carter felt it was his duty to help them out, for a fee of course.

Justin was supposed to pay him twenty-grand, and so far, he hadn't transferred the money. Carter hung up the phone which had rung over fifteen times and quickly went online and checked his bank account just to be sure. *Still no money. Dammit.*

No wonder the man was screening his calls. *Asshole.*

He shut the banking app and went back to his list. There were a few others he needed to light a fire under and give a gentle reminder, but he wasn't going to give up on Finch, even if he had to drive up to Michigan to find him.

He hoped it didn't come to that. Justin could be a mean son of a gun, and he should have thought of that before he did him any favors.

He scrolled to the bottom of the list and shook his head as another name popped out at him. "Ken Sin."

CHAPTER 6

DAREK

The morning had turned crazy with Darek going to check on Lizzy. As they lay in bed at her house, Darek looked around the room, wondering why they hadn't spent more time there. He'd only been to the apartment once or twice, and before then, hadn't made it that far inside. He'd stood at the door, walked into the bathroom once, but never stayed. The place was really plain and seemed more like a bachelor's pad than his own. Lizzy liked things pretty basic, from what he could tell, and he was surprised to see that even though she'd lived in that apartment for some time that he knew of, there were still boxes upon boxes piled up in what should be her dining area.

The cat, which she'd affectionately called Bob, jumped up on the bed and crawled up between Darek's feet to sit and lick himself.

"Do you have to do that here, buddy?" He put the cat on the floor and rolled over to face Lizzy. "I should get back to work."

She was staring at the wall over his shoulder, lost in deep thought until his words seemed to bring her around. "Yeah, rub it in why don't you?" She reached forward and stroked his cheek.

"I'm sorry," he said, bringing her hand to his lips. "But you know it's for the best. Better not poke the bear that is Sam Reed."

"Whatever." She got to her feet and gave him a kiss. "While you go, I think I'll take a shower. Don't let the cat out."

"Fine, kick me out just like that. You'll miss me." He gave a wink as she went into the bathroom, and then he got to his feet, put on his pants, and prepared to head back to the office. He had calls to make, and now that lunch was over, he hoped that Carter would be available to chat.

"What does a pastor do on Mondays?" he asked the cat as it followed him to the door. He didn't want to pick it up but knew if he didn't want the cat to dart out of the door, he needed to. He made sure he had his keys and then picked up Bob, who furiously tried to scratch him with no luck. As he walked out the door, he looked down at the poor beast's paws and noticed he lacked the tools to draw blood. "Nice, try, fucker." He tossed the cat back into the room and shut the door. "Not today, buddy. You get to take care of your master."

He walked out to his car and took out his phone, dialing Carter's number. It was time to get back to work, and he might as well jump in with both feet.

Carter answered with the sound of busy traffic in the distance. "Hello? Can you hear me?"

"Yeah, I hear you," said Darek, getting into his own car. "It's Darek. Can you hear me?"

"Darek Blake? I didn't expect to hear from you. The signal was a little fuzzy for a moment, but I'm driving back to the Church from my lunch date."

Darek wondered who the man had for lunch and if his wife was still away as she had been. "I'm doing the same. I've meant to call you. I have a couple of things you need to know, and I wanted to ask a favor."

Carter chuckled. "Bad news and a favor, huh? My two least favorite things."

"Yeah, well, the bad news isn't my fault." He tried to think of a better way to tell him than just blurting it out, but there wasn't one. "Justin Finch is dead." He took a breath and let that sink in a second. "I talked to Brandy, and she told me that he was the victim of a random home invasion."

"Dammit. It figures." Carter sounded as if Justin's death was a huge inconvenience.

Darek was shocked by the reaction. "Is something wrong?" He slowed his car to make a turn onto the main road.

Carter's voice fell. "Yes, Justin owed me money. Guess I won't be seeing it now."

Darek thought that was a little strange. "You loaned him money? He was loaded, wasn't he?"

"It wasn't like that. I performed a service. Church business."

"I see," said Darek, knowing he shouldn't pry. But it did seem curious. He'd have to feel him out if he could get him there in person. "I do have another bit of bad news, by the way, before we get to the favor. It seems the shooting in New Orleans was a hit. One of the men arrested has run his mouth to the other cellmates, including an informant. He said that it was a hit."

"Someone fucking paid them to shoot at you?"

"Yeah, any idea who? I'm assuming that their intended target was there, but what if you and Ethan were supposed to be among us? You could have very easily been killed."

"I've thanked God every day since that wasn't the case." Carter's voice sounded sincere enough, but Darek wasn't too sure.

"Do you have anyone in your life that might want you dead?" It was worth asking, seeing how he could have easily been with them that night.

"No, people adore me," said Carter in an unconvincing tone.

Darek switched lanes on the freeway, checking his mirrors while thinking of his next words. "I think that someone could have organized the hit to take the heat off themselves. It wouldn't be the first time the killer had someone else do their dirty work."

"So, what's the favor?" asked Carter as the sound of a shutting car door came through the phone. The noise of the traffic had stopped.

"As I mentioned before, we've got Ken Sin locked up here. My superior wants me to investigate him further, dig into his religious affiliations, and talk to anyone who has counseled him in the past."

"I told you, Darek, I didn't really know him that well. I'd rather not be dragged down to New York with this kind of nonsense. I mean, I'd like to help, but I'm not sure it would. Whatever crazy scheme he cooked up, he's done it on his own."

"My boss doesn't care about that; he just needs me to make a show that we're doing all we can." He knew it was time to feed Carter's ego. That was the only way you could get the man to do anything. "He wants a man of your stature and fame to step in and be an advisor of sorts. Anything you could bring to the table would be welcome."

"Well, I usually receive compensation for my assistance."

"The PD and FBI don't work that way."

"The FBI?" Darek could tell that he had Carter's attention. "You know, it might look good if I were providing a service to my country and its people if I worked with the FBI to bring justice to this case. But I'd need your word that nothing from our past comes out while I'm there. I can't have this coming back to bite me in the ass when word of what happened in Virginia comes out."

"That's never going to happen. Bay and I are already in over our heads, and maybe it's time some of you other men step up to the plate and help us figure this shit out. That's why we had the meeting in the first place. So we could band together and make sure we all survive this mess."

"And yet, two more of us have died since the meeting, which hasn't even been but a couple of weeks ago."

"I'm aware. But there isn't any proof that the killer has anything to do with their deaths." Darek hoped to prove it, but that wasn't a given. It could very well have been a random crime that took out both men.

Carter let out a sigh. "Normally, I'd jump at the chance to get away from this place, but as it turns out, I find myself in a bit of a pickle."

Darek knew the asshole was going to have some sort of excuse, but he was ready to play his trump card. "I don't care about your pickle. I need you here. That should be enough reason to come. I've never asked you for anything."

"It's important to you, isn't it? Let me guess, you have to impress someone, and I'm what you impress them with?"

Darek rolled his eyes at the gall of the asshole whose ego was going to get the best of him one day. "Yeah, that's it. I need your help. Are you going to come or not? I can call someone else; I just thought you might be better since you actually know the man and can stir some kind of emotion in him." And if Darek was lucky, Sin might slam Carter face-first into a table.

"I wasn't just making excuses about my situation. I've already missed quite a bit of work with trips lately, and there's trouble at the office. Financial in nature. It would be a bad time to leave, but I'll see what I can do. Don't go calling anyone else just yet."

Darek had hoped he wouldn't have to wait for an answer. "Fine, but I need to know something as soon as possible."

Carter sighed. "Okay, I'll let you know." He went quiet for a moment. "I can't believe it about Justin."

Darek tried to gauge the sincerity in his voice. "Yeah, you know him and Brandy were going to try and make it work between them. I guess death brings some people closer. She said she's pregnant with Corey's child."

"The lord *does* work in mysterious ways. I'm sure there is a reason for all of this, though I admit it sure as hell doesn't seem like it. It's just a damned shame."

"I agree." Darek hated to think of Brandy and the stress she'd endured so early on in her pregnancy. It was a wonder she didn't miscarry.

"I wondered if you had her number," Carter said. "I'd sure like to talk to her and maybe offer some counsel. I've handled many situations like hers through the years, and I think I could be of some comfort. Perhaps offer her some assistance of some kind."

Darek hesitated a little. He had her number from when they were in New Orleans and he'd wanted to check on Corey. While he usually didn't give out people's numbers to just anyone, he didn't see the harm in letting Carter call and offer his condolences. "Sure. I'll text it to you. I don't think she'd mind, and she might like to know that we care.

She and Corey were head over heels, and I can't imagine how it must feel to lose Justin so soon after." He thought it was rather odd, but stranger things had happened, and he had no reason to doubt her word, especially since it was something so easily confirmed.

"Thanks so much. I really loved both of those men. You know I used to think that Justin was born in the wrong century. He would have been more at home in the eighteen-hundreds than today."

Darek smiled. "Yeah, they were both good guys." He thought of how Corey had wanted it all to end with him. But now, they were both gone. "Do you ever think that we're next?"

Carter was quiet for a moment. "I know when my time comes, I'll be ready for the good lord to take me home."

There was something in those words that didn't sound the least bit true, and he had the strange feeling that despite them, Carter was just as afraid to die as anyone else. Perhaps he knew he had a much worse fate awaiting? Darek hoped to find out. If only Carter would come. The only other way to get him there was to subpoena him, and he really hoped it didn't come to that. He'd save that threat for another time when it was absolutely necessary.

"I just think it's crazy. How we're all leaving this world. I don't want to be next. I have too much I want to do, you know?"

"Unfortunately, Darek, it doesn't work that way. The good Lord will call us home when it's our time, regardless of the circumstance."

Darek shook his head. He just couldn't believe it. "I don't think the good lord has anything to do with us dropping like flies. No, that's the work of evil. The work of a trained killer."

"Or the devil," said Carter. "Either way, God's allowed it to happen. It's his will."

"Then forgive me, Pastor Hamilton, but if that's true, then God sucks." He just couldn't see that all of those years ago, the twelve of them met only to be picked off in order of their astrological signs. Only a calculated madman could make that happen.

CHAPTER 7

CARTER

Carter hung up the phone and got out of his car. He and Darek had finally finished their long conversation, and while it let him know about a lot of things happening, the one thing he was focused on was Justin's death.

Not that he had been killed, but that he had been killed before he had a chance to pay Carter what he owed. He waited a few minutes as he walked to his office, and sure enough, Darek made good on his promise to give him Brandy's phone number.

He knew that the papers he signed and mailed were designed to make Brandy look like Corey's widow, and with the man being responsible for one of the hottest gaming apps out there, he knew she had come into some money on that alone.

He needed her to know that he was still there with his hand out, and he had every intention of asking for more than the tiny twenty-thousand Justin had offered. He had only gone along with his scheme because he liked Justin and knew better than to fuck with him, but with him out of the picture and no one there to protect Brandy, he could go in for the kill and make her pay millions.

It was simple. She could pay up or lose it all.

He walked into his office, ignoring Peggy who told him Eddie had wanted him to call. He didn't have time for more church melodrama when he had a chance at tapping into that kind of cash. Cash that could more than secure his place at the head of the church, or even better, money that he could build a new life on if everything crumbled.

He pulled out his phone and dialed the number but got no answer. He did, however, get a chance to leave a message. "This is Carter Hamilton, a close friend of Justin's whom you're going to need to contact right away. It's regarding your recent nuptials which I performed in New Orleans." He hung up the phone and hoped she realized how important it was to get in touch with him.

It would be easy to blow it off, but one call and her little game was over.

Before he could situate at his desk, he heard footsteps down the hall. The familiar sound of high heels and short steps told him there was a woman approaching. He straightened his tie and slicked back his hair, and when he looked up, he saw Keely poke her head around the door and smile.

"Hi, Carter. I hope I'm not interrupting your busy day." She stepped in and shut the door behind her, turning the lock.

"I've only just gotten back to work from lunch, so you have caught me just in time. I'm about to have to make a few phone calls." He didn't want the woman lingering around his office too much, especially dressed the way she was. He let his gaze linger down her body, taking in every curve beneath her tight blouse and skirt, all the way down to her fuck-me pumps.

"I'm so sorry. I guess I should get right to the point. You see, my rent is due tomorrow, and I don't get paid until next week. I was hoping my ex would take care of it since it's still leased in his name and he's supposed to be handling it, but he didn't. He said it was time I start taking care of myself, which would be fine normally, but he didn't give me any warning. I'm so afraid that I'm going to lose my house, and I hoped the church could help me. I just need a loan until payday."

Carter had heard it all before, and while he knew she was going through a tough time, a member had to be a member for longer than the few months she'd been going to the church to qualify for assistance. And not only that, there was a process in place for such things. "I'm sorry, Keely. I know it's tough. We have some steps we take in offering assistance. You'll have to go and see Peggy, my secretary. She can help you file the papers with the financial office, and since you're not quite a six-month member, I'll be sure to put in a special request for you."

"Wait," she said, her expression changing to annoyed confusion. "I don't need financial aid; I came to you hoping you'd help me out. I mean, I know it's probably not the way things are done, but I could offer you a service, and you could pay me. Say three hundred cash?"

Carter tried to control his expression and didn't want the woman to think he was laughing at her, but there was a snowball's chance in hell that he'd just hand over money to anyone, much less pay three hundred dollars for a blow job, no matter how good it was. "I'm sorry, Keely. I just don't have that on me personally."

She rose from her seat and walked around to the other side of the desk. "Then how about we take a little ride to the bank? I could reach over and help you work your stick." She gave him a sexy smile, and he had a feeling she wasn't going to take no for an answer. How he handled the situation was going to define a lot of things, but one thing was for sure. He no longer had the upper hand. She had come asking, knowing there was no way he could refuse her. Not because she was so irresistible but because she was another woman who he had fucked in his congregation and she could make waves. Especially now that the deacons and elders were all up his ass and in his business.

"I can't leave, but I'll let you provide that service now, and I'll give you the two hundred I have in my pocket. You can earn the rest tomorrow if you're a good girl." He ran his hand up her skirt and cupped her ass cheek, giving it a pinch. He let his hand slip down, rubbing her through her lace panties which grew wet beneath his fingers.

"Fine, but I want to come too." She stepped forward and straddled his lap, putting her big breasts in his face as she reached down and undid his pants. Once she had his cock out, he put his hands around her waist and guided her down on his dick.

"I'll make you come then you can suck me off. I want to come down that pretty throat." Less mess, he thought. His fucking day was messy enough.

"I could be your private whore, you know? Make sure all of your needs are met."

"You already are, aren't you? I mean, you will be as soon as you take my money." He was good with that. What he wasn't good with was this becoming a habit. Sex and secrets were usually expensive though, at least from his experience. She could cost him thousands easily.

He had to give her credit; she was working hard for her dollar. She slowly rocked her hips, and when she made a little moaning sound, he captured her lips with his to keep her quiet. He felt her walls tighten, milking his cock as she came. She stilled, and he pulled away, putting a finger to his lips. "We can't be loud in here, angel."

"It feels so good." She hopped off and got to her feet, straightening her skirt as she got to her knees.

He reached forward and put his hand around the back of her neck, guiding her down, and once she had her mouth around his head, he closed his eyes and rocked his hips upward, pulling her down. He knew exactly how much of his dick she could take, and he wasn't going to stop forcing until his balls were at her lips.

She held herself there, puffing as the girth became too much, and he pulled away and let her take her time, sucking and licking. He finally felt his orgasm on the horizon and put both hands on the side of her face and held her still. Then he rocked his hips upward, fucking her face and throat until he orgasmed, splashing her tongue and coating her throat. She gulped it down like a pro and pulled away with a smile.

As one hand wiped her mouth, she held the other out, wanting her pay. "Do you think I'll be able to earn the rest tonight instead? I have work tomorrow."

"No, it's too risky. And no more office pop-ins. I'll meet you somewhere on our lunch hour."

She nodded. "Okay." She rubbed her fingers together, and he reached into his wallet and pulled out two crisp hundreds. "Thank you," she said, snatching them out of his hands.

"This can't be a habit, Keely. If I get caught doing this, it not only means the well runs dry, but it means that we have to stop having our fun. You feel me?"

She gave a nod and licked her lips. "Don't worry. I'm good with it. I just needed a little help."

He gave her a pat on the bottom, and she walked around the desk and grabbed her bag. "I'll see you tomorrow."

When she was about to open the door to leave, the phone rang, and he looked down to see that it was the number he had for Brandy. *Time to make more fun money.*

He answered. "It was wise of you to call me back, Mrs. Farrow." He hoped the name bothered her and would put her on edge, but she didn't seem too fazed.

"I take it you're the person who Justin talked to about faking the marriage certificate?"

"Justin called me about performing your ceremony with Corey," he said.

"And what did he promise you in return?"

"My usual fee," said Carter. "But in light of things, I think my rates just increased."

"Of course, it did." The amused tone went out of her voice. "How much do you want?"

"I know what Corey was worth. I can imagine that increasing the original amount by twenty would be a start, but then, you could do better."

"That's not helpful. You see, Justin didn't tell me how much he offered you to start."

"Twenty-grand. But I'm thinking more like two million, maybe five. I know your late husband had more money than he knew what to do with."

"I think you're grossly overestimating his worth."

"No, I don't think so. There was insurance money on top of his already insane bankroll. I'll make it easy. I want half. Don't pay me, and I'll make sure the FBI knows you faked the marriage certificate and you'll lose all of it and go to prison for fraud."

Brandy gave a nervous laugh. "You're out of your mind. I have a baby to think about. Do I need to remind you of the details in this situation? Your name is on the document too; you'd be just as guilty."

"The signature is a forgery, and I'm an upstanding citizen. That can be proved. Maybe it was done by Justin before you had him killed?"

"I beg your pardon?" Her tone hardened, and Carter laughed, knowing he was going to have a lot of fun with her.

"I think it's quite a coincidence that two men who were trying to take care of you end up dead," he said. "And you sure didn't take long to rebound from Corey. Poor guy's ashes were still embers when you put your claws into Justin Finch."

"I'll get you your money so you can fuck off. I never want to hear from you again."

"I'll have the account set up later today and text you the number."

Her breath sent static through the phone, and he realized she was in tears. "I loved Corey. We had big plans until someone gunned him down in the street like a dog. I'll have to live the rest of my life alone, knowing that someone killed him and took him from me and the baby."

"And you'll do it all while living in style I'm sure. Save your sob tears, honey." He didn't want to hear it. "Have the money there by the end of the day." With that, he hung up and eased back in his chair. He knew he had to figure out an answer for Darek, but he was going to make sure that none of the other Zodiacs knew a damned thing about what he had planned. Bay had told them to seize their fortune in life, and that was exactly what he was about to do.

CHAPTER 8

BAY

Bay hadn't heard from Mia in nearly a week, and he was losing all hope of finding her alive. He had checked with everyone he could think of and had even given himself a few days past when he knew he should tell Lila and the girls' mother that she'd gone missing.

He hadn't let anything affect him for as long as he could remember, and while he was very much in touch with anger, this emotion was something different, and that was very rare and frustrating for him.

He hated to compare it to the way he felt about Rose Marie, but it certainly wasn't the type of feeling he had for Lila. This was separate and too complicated to deal with. A part of him felt it might just serve him right to love her, and if there was a God, he was probably laughing in Bay's face, knowing he took her away from him.

But there wasn't a God, only himself, and he wasn't going to let this knock him down. He raised his glass to his lips and drank the last swig of his bourbon. Then he went to fetch another one.

He had never been a coward in his life, but telling Lila about her sister? He needed a lot of liquid courage to make that call.

As he walked to the kitchen, he heard the soft hum of the security camera moving and then the sound of his alert beeping to let him know there was movement from a potential intruder. He took out his phone and pulled up his camera feeds, and sure enough, there was something moving out by the pool house.

Bay went for the gun he kept in a box on the fireplace mantle and checked to make sure it was loaded.

It hadn't escaped his attention that the number of Zodiacs was decreasing, and while he'd never admit it bothered him to anyone else, he had grown increasingly concerned for his safety. He knew that by all accounts, Carter should be up next on the chopping block, but there was never any guarantee with homicidal maniacs. He should know.

He held the gun tight and hurried to the back-patio door where he could have access to the pool area. He hoped this intruder would be acting alone. He didn't want someone to come up behind him on his way out and take him down.

He looked out to the trellis beside the house, and it was moving, the entire thing shaking like it could break any minute. As he moved out, hoping to walk up behind them, he saw a little shadow moving across the roof. They were headed for the upstairs window.

His heart raced, and he ran back into the house to head them off. He had the strangest feeling come into his chest again as he took to the stairs.

Running down the hall, he threw open Mia's bedroom door, and sure enough, his instinct had been correct. She fell into the window and landed on the floor.

Bay rushed over to pick her up.

"I'm fine!" she said, scrambling to her feet.

He held on to her arm and checked her over. "You're not all right. Where the hell have you been?"

Mia pulled away and walked over to the bed. "I had to get away and think."

"Think? You had to think? You can fucking think any time of the day. All you had to do was pick up a phone and fucking tell me you needed to think." He threw his hands up in the air and started to pace the room. "Do you have any idea how fucking worried I've been about you? That you were lying someplace dead in the gutter or tossed into the river?" He had feared all the evil things he'd done to others had been done to her.

"I'm sorry. I just, I—" She began to sob, and Bay resisted the urge to hold her. He wanted to pull her into his arms and cradle her like a child and kiss her feverishly like a lover, but then a part of him wanted to show her the pain she'd shown him. He closed the window and then turned to face her.

"I know about your affair with Maxwell Smith."

She backed away even more, looking as if Bay might strike her at any moment. "I'm sorry." Tears sprang to her eyes.

"You're a grown woman, Mia. You're certainly entitled to make mistakes and to have affairs. What you do with your body is not my choice. I do not own you." As much as he wanted to, he hadn't ever. "I tried to keep you pure and innocent for my own ego. You were, to me, unlike any other."

"I'm sorry I let you down."

"I guess it's my fault for thinking you could have feelings for me. I know I'm a rough man. Hard to handle. I've always been just that. Only Rose Marie could tame me when I was a boy, and I misbehaved for everyone else but her."

Mis shook her head slowly. "It's not that, though, Bay. It's just I was so angry that you wouldn't let me have my fun, and it didn't seem fair."

"Why would you think I treat you unfairly when I give you everything?" His voice had gotten much louder than he expected, and when Mia flinched, he knew he should tone it down or risk losing her forever. He had to be calm and coaxing.

"You get to eat your cake and have it too."

"Because I take it, Mia."

"I realized after I rebelled that I only did it because I love you."

He was about to scold her for using such a line on him, but then a closer look at her expression told him it was true. He felt such relief that he closed his eyes.

"I didn't mean to disappoint you, Bay. I've just been dealing with my feelings. I thought I could just have fun with how things were. I liked being your little kitten, your plaything to be petted and adored. But as my feelings got stronger, I knew it was all for nothing. You'll never be mine, Bay. You'll always be Lila's. She's giving you a child. How could I compete with that? How could my feelings matter at all compared to hers? I know you could never really love me back."

"Why did you sneak in?"

"I only meant to come and get a few things. I am staying with a friend."

"I've called all of your friends."

"I know. I had her lie." She lowered her chin. "I'll just gather my things and leave."

"No, you won't. For one, you don't sneak into my house and tell me how I feel and who I am. And secondly, you are not safe out on the streets with some little liar who should have had the good sense to tell me the fucking truth before I involved the police." He narrowed his eyes. "Did Max know where you went?"

She shook her head. "No, it wasn't about him. I broke things off. He was okay, but it was too weird for me."

"Too weird?" Bay couldn't imagine it getting any fucking weirder than it had been with him. "Did he do something inappropriate?"

"He liked it rough, and he always wanted me to beg. He wanted me to look in his eyes and put his hands on my throat while I begged. I nearly passed out once, and when I asked him not to do it again, he got even weirder. Told me that I should be used to weird shit after fucking you."

Bay wasn't too shocked by the officer's strange fetishes. As the owner of a sex club, he had seen plenty, but what pissed him off more than anything was the manner in which he liked to get off. Bay didn't like anyone abusing his property, human or otherwise.

"What do you mean even weirder?"

"The last time we met, he had this knife, and he held it to me, said he wanted me to pretend he was going to kill me. It was too intense. I didn't mind fucking. He was actually a lot smaller than I'm used to, so it wasn't all that bad. But the creepy shit that went with it was too much to take."

"I hope you realize what kind of things you'll find when you go out looking for better."

"There isn't anyone better," she said. "I've learned that."

"Then why are you planning on leaving again?"

"Because you're not mine, and you never will be."

"Greedy girl. Isn't it enough to be mine? I treated you like a princess, pampered you, gave you the world, and you shit on me by going to that cop!"

"He approached me," she said. "I just felt so flattered."

"I'll kill that asshole. Preying on young girls." He knew some could say the same of him, but Mia was his family.

Mia lowered her eyes to his feet. "Are you going to punish me?"

He walked over and lifted her chin so she could meet his eyes. "You have a lot to do to make up for this, Mia. Are you up for the task?"

Her tears came swiftly again, rolling down her cheeks. "Yes. Thank you."

"No, thank you, Mia. Thank you for loving me." He pulled her close, tightening his grip on her arm. "But if you ever lie to me again, I'll throw you out and disown you. You'll not be allowed near Lila or the baby, and I'll even make sure your mother doesn't respond. Do you understand what I'm saying, Mia?"

"Yes, sir." She began to cry, and Bay wondered if he was choosing the right thing. He really thought it possible that he loved her as much as she loved him. He just didn't know how to show it. His love was possessive and harsh; it wasn't the kind of love that other men could give her. But shame for her, she was too good for other men. He was going to keep her all to himself.

"You know, I think we should go get you cleaned up, and I'll bring you to bed. We have a lot of making up to do." He pulled her close and kissed her forehead. Then he walked her to the master suite where his large marble tub and shower were about to be put to use in more ways than one.

As she pulled off her clothes, she kept a melancholy look, like any minute he would rip the carpet out from under her and things would go south. "Chin up, baby. It's not many days I give someone a second chance."

The two of them moved together until their bodies were joined. Bay kissed her hard, knowing he'd have to do all he could to reclaim what had once been his, but that aching feeling in his chest had slowly begun to subside, with pleasure filling its place.

CHAPTER 9

DAREK

"They've found Antonio," said Lizzy, walking out to greet him at his car with her morning coffee in hand. She took a sip as Darek gave her a strange look and closed his car door.

"Antonio?"

"Yes," she said, rolling her eyes. "Come on, I sat around stuffing my face with enough sugar to be comatose yesterday, and you're the one who can't remember the fine details of the case?"

"Ah, the tattoo," said Darek, remembering the victim's wrist. "Did they find him dead or alive?"

"Alive and he's not talking. Yet. They arrested him on drug charges, so he'll be around a while, no matter the outcome of our little chat."

They turned and headed for the building where Darek wondered how far into processing the man was. "How soon will they have him ready for us?"

Lizzy placed her hand on his shoulder. "They just snagged him an hour ago. They are a bit behind, but I told them to move him up. I want him in stripes before I see him, and I don't want to wait all goddamned morning."

"Do you think it's going to tie into our case?" he asked. Just because it was a brutal stabbing didn't mean it was linked.

She gave a shrug. "Unless someone thought it was a good idea to throw us off by using a similar knife."

Darek stepped up ahead of her and opened the door. "That's true. Maybe we'll get a miracle, and he'll say Ken Sin put him up to it." He gave a chuckle, knowing that was never going to happen.

"He could. People watch the news, and with them sensationalizing Sin's arrest, a natural cult following could form. Stranger things have happened for sure."

"Like a man saying he's a serial killer for fame?"

Lizzy rolled her eyes and sighed. "Yeah, just like that."

As they walked into the front office, Lizzy let out a sigh. "It's good to be home," she said, being a little dramatic.

Darek shook his head, not understanding her one bit. "Are you serious? I'd do anything for someone to give me a day off."

"I could smash your face into a table if you want," she said with a nudge.

Darek glanced over at her bruises, which were healing and turning an ugly shade of purple with yellow edges. The brown was gone, which was good. It showed that she was healing. "No thanks."

"Trust me; I wouldn't wish this on anyone. I know people think I'm a battered wife."

Darek gave her an apologetic look. "Yeah, they think I did it. I've had some dirty looks."

Darek's phone rang on the way to the office, and seeing it was Bay, he decided to step into the men's room as Lizzy continued on to the office. "What's an early morning Bay Collins got for me?"

"Good news this time," said Bay. "Mia is home, safe and sound. I thought I should call off the dogs."

He sounded alive again, almost like he was smiling, and Darek could imagine the devilish grin. "I know you're relieved. Don't be too hard on her." He couldn't imagine what he might put Mia through.

"All is good in my kingdom," said Bay.

"Well, let's hope it stays that way. I'm about to question the boyfriend of that girl they found. She was stabbed multiple times, and Cobb is still checking on the type of blade that was used to see if match's the other killings."

"Do you think our killer did it?"

Darek hated the way that sounded. "Our killer" was only a reminder that their turn in front of the firing squad was approaching fast if they didn't figure out who it was. He shook his head. "I don't know. Oh, there's something else I needed to tell you."

Bay gave a sound of disappointment. "Not bad news, I hope. We were on such a roll."

"I've called Carter and asked him to come out. My boss wants me to dig into Sin's mind a bit and wanted to know if he had maybe gotten the idea from some type of religious influence."

"Ah, I remember our friend claiming that he knew him. I bet he's kicking himself for that little confession."

"He didn't sound too impressed about coming to New York, but he's checking his schedule, and he's supposed to get back with me."

Bay laughed. "There's no way he's going to come willingly; you might have to force him. Whatever you do, make sure he knows to keep his mouth shut. We don't need him to let on to you two knowing each other."

"Yeah, I'm aware. I'm getting good at this game." He had sure played it for long enough.

Bay laughed. "Well, just don't get too cocky. That's when mistakes are made, my friend."

"I'll let you know what happens with that. But when he's in town, I want us to get together with him, maybe bend his ear about the New Orleans shooting."

"I'm game. Give me a call. It will be nice to see Carter again. You know, it could be the last time. I mean, with him being on the chopping block, he might just be dead in another week."

"Don't say that."

"Why? You don't want to bring bad luck down on us or something? It's a little too late for that."

"Right. I'll hit you up when I know something." Darek ended the call and then went back to the office where he found Lizzy and Max talking at the coffee bar.

When she turned around and saw him, she hurried over. "They're ready for us. And I got a call from Dr. Cobb. The knife marks do not match the same blade that the killer used. The blade was serrated, which is why it did a lot more damage to the tissue even though there weren't as many entry wounds."

"Was there any other kind of marks on her? Tattoos of the zodiac? Something carved into her skin?"

"Nope, nothing. But the stab wounds weren't the only thing they found. She had blunt force trauma to the head, and Cobb took his time to make sure that it was the initial blow."

"So, she was hit with something?" Darek asked. "Before she was killed?"

"Either that or she fell and hit her head, but he did say it's more consistent with someone being struck than falling. And she also had some older wounds. Bruising and some evidence of past injuries. Some were as recent as ten months ago."

"She's been abused?" he asked. Lizzy nodded as he continued. "So maybe this asshole finally fucked up and killed her." Darek had seen so many domestic abuse cases in his time. It was something he never got used to, and it oftentimes ended with the abuser accidentally killing or seriously injuring their spouse.

"Well, we'll get to ask the asshole." Lizzy walked over and took another sip of her coffee. "They said they're almost ready with him." She took her cup across the room and tossed it in the trash as Darek prepared to go.

"Come on, let's get this over with. The victim's name was Sarah Beth. Let's make sure to use it a lot." Lizzy let out a sigh, and Darek wondered if she were nervous going in to meet with another man that might get violent.

As they walked into the room, Darek walked over to the guard. "This time, make sure to cuff him to the table. I don't want to take any chances with this asshole."

The man nodded, and minutes later when they brought him in, they secured his cuffs to the table.

He was covered in tattoos, his face looking like someone got carried away doodling, and the sour look on his face gave away his personality.

Lizzy walked over and sat down, not bothering to keep her chair back like Darek wished she would. The man looked like a rabid grizzly bear compared to Ken Sin, and he'd done enough damage. Instead, she seemed to make a point of moving her chair close to show she wasn't at all intimidated by the asshole.

"Antonio Mendez," said Lizzy.

"Smart bitch, glad you can read." He gave a cocky smile and looked down his nose at her.

Lizzy didn't let his mouth faze her. "I can also read that this isn't your first arrest. Seems you have a history of drugs and violence. There are domestic assault charges on your file. That explains your girlfriend's medical records."

The man's dead stare was unaffected. He had to be a monster compared to the small woman they'd found.

"You like to beat on little girls?" asked Darek. "Think it makes you a man?"

"I didn't hit that little bitch." He turned his nose up.

"Did you stab Sarah Beth?" asked Lizzy, leaning forward toward Antonio.

"Who hit you?" asked Antonio. "Was it your husband?" He turned his head, and a slow smile spread his lips.

"You think this is funny?" Darek had the urge to beat his ass. There wasn't anything humorous about the girl's mutilation. "I think you did kill Sarah Beth. And I think if you did, your best option would be to tell us. Show the judge you can have some kind of remorse."

The smile left his face. "Why you putting this on me? There's a killer out there in the city stabbing people. How do you know this isn't him?"

Lizzy gave him a sideward look. "Is that what you want us to believe, Antonio? Is that why you cut Sarah Beth up?"

He turned and shook his head. "I didn't cut her up."

"No?" asked Darek.

"No." His eyes turned to Darek's so fast that he felt it.

"You beat her up though, didn't you?" Lizzy eased back in her chair. "You went a little far. Sarah Beth cracked her head on the floor. You realized how bad it was, that she probably wouldn't make it, and so you needed to cover it up."

The man clammed up, and Darek knew she had him. "You found it easy to put the blame on someone else, so you stabbed her, finishing her off."

He shook his head. "She was already dead."

"No, see, that's where you're wrong. Sarah Beth wasn't dead, Antonio. Stunned, unconscious, yes. But not dead. There was still hope. Still a chance to save her, but you didn't know that."

"She was dead!" he shouted, his voice booming.

"The blood shows she was still alive. She bled out. Blood reacts differently when a deceased person is stabbed. There is no heart pumping to push the blood through the veins, to make the type of patterns we saw on her face and clothing."

Antonio reached up and wiped a single tear that pooled in the corner of his eye. "I thought she was dead. There was no pulse. My friend had told me about the murders. I thought it was my best chance."

Darek breathed a sigh of relief, and Lizzy met his eyes. He had thought for sure that this idiot would put it all on the killer, but somewhere in him, he had a conscience.

Lizzy got up and stood over the man, resting her palms flat against the table. "At least she's at peace now. No more coming home to a monster like you. What are you going to do with yourself now that you can't beat on her? You see, we're going to lock you up and you'll have to face men who will knock you around. And every time one of their fists connects, and you feel that pain, I want you to remember this face." Lizzy tossed out a few crime scene photos.

Instead, the man leaned in closer. "You sound like you speak from experience. Tell me, who beat on you? Was it your daddy? Husband? I bet you took it real good. I bet both of your old men put it to you hard and beat that ass."

Lizzy lunged forward, but Darek managed to grab her from behind and pull her away as she wailed like a cat in heat and kicked and screamed. Darek picked her up and took her away, only putting her down on both feet when he had her in the hallway.

"What the fuck was that about?" he shouted. He could hear the man's laughter in the next room. "You let that asshole get the best of you back there."

Lizzy spun around and pushed him, but then she stood there, panting.

"Get yourself together. I think Reed was right to send you home yesterday. I think you need another day to cool your heels. What got into you?"

"Assholes like him deserve to be brutalized."

Darek had never heard that tone come out of her mouth, and he narrowed his eyes, wondering if she really had been speaking from experience. He pushed her back down the hall as the guards took care of Antonio and was glad that hadn't taken any longer than it did. They had their confession, and best of all, the case didn't connect with theirs. That bought him a bit more time to try and figure out who the killer was and do what Reed had asked.

Now, if he could keep Lizzy from cracking up, he'd be doing good.

CHAPTER 10

CARTER

Carter leaned back in his chair and pulled out the top drawer of his desk where he kept his planner. With nothing else on the schedule, he had no excuse not to go and see Darek and Ken Sin. Part of him wanted out of it; another part knew going away at a time like this wasn't going to make his life any easier when he came back.

He picked up his phone and dialed Darek's number. The man answered after one ring. "Carter?" he said with a surprised tone.

"Yeah, it's me. I've called to tell you I'll come up and see you, but I wanted to know if this is going to be a private meeting or will your partner be there? Anyone else?"

"Why, is there something I should know?"

Carter wondered if he should tell him exactly how well he knew Ken.

"Look," said Darek. "I'm just going to say this. You need to make sure you tell me everything. If there was more to the relationship with you and this man, I need to know it."

"Everyone knew Ken was some kind of washed-up rockstar when he showed up at the church, and since we've been televised, we've had all sorts show up wanting to be on our stage. I listened to his testimony, and while I wasn't too sure that he was truly sincere, I knew a lot of the staff and members really thought he was a changed man."

"So he was a celebrity guest?"

"Somewhat. It always looks good when you can get someone who people have heard of, who had been through hell and are looking for redemption. The crowd eats it up. If they see that God's worked a miracle in their life, then they are more likely to have faith that he will do some great thing with their own. The harder the testimony, the harder the climb from the pits of hell, the better. I saw great potential in Sin. I mean, hell, the name alone would be enough to make a good pitch. Ken Sin no more. Could you imagine the marketing?"

"So, you were closer to him than you let on," said Darek.

Carter let out a long breath. "Yes. I befriended him. I tried to get him to see the light, but then I learned that he was just playing the church for attention. He became obsessed with me and my reputation and wanted to have something like that of his own."

"Jesus. You should have told me before, Carter." Darek's disappointment was clear in his tone.

"I just need to know that our past won't come into it," said Carter. "And I need to let you know that while I didn't say what we did, I did talk extensively to him about how one person could lead a group of people to do unspeakable things." He figured Darek would know where he'd learned that. Bay Collins

"Did you tell him anything about your own past sins?" Darek's voice took on an accusing tone.

"I never gave him specifics, Darek."

"You have to understand how crazy this is to me. With him stepping up as the Zodiac and then knowing you. You're the one who encouraged his behavior."

"I wouldn't go that far, Darek." He let out a sigh. "Look, we'll talk more about it when I get there. I've got to go and break the news to my staff and make my reservations. I'll tell them that I'm going to work with the NYPD, and hopefully, they won't give me too much shit about it."

"I'll see you soon," said Darek. "But we're going to finish this conversation."

Hopefully, by then, he could make up his mind about what to say. He didn't want Darek to know about the times he and Sin had sneaked off to clubs and went drinking in another town; the times the man had managed to get him out of his shell. It was then he'd let too much spill.

He ended the call and got to his feet. He walked over to the door that connected his office to Peggy's and opened it just enough to stick his head into the room. "I'm leaving for New York as soon as I can get a flight out. I'll need you to contact Eddie and tell him I've got no choice. I know he's not going to be happy, but when the NYPD calls, you respond. I've been asked to go and meet with Ken Sin."

Peggy turned to face him with an expression that made him look as if she'd sucked a lemon. "Ken Sin? That washed up rocker who came to our church?"

"Yes, he's the one. He's been arrested in a high-profile case, and naturally, they want a high-profile pastor to come and counsel with him. They think I might be able to offer some insight."

"Insight? Will you tell them how he got pissed and left after you wouldn't let him preach a Sunday service?"

Carter hadn't even mentioned that to Darek, but there was so much about Ken that he'd tried to put out of his head. "No, I'm not going to make it personal. They've asked me to a job, and I'm doing it." He wanted to make it sound as professional as possible so the elders and deacons couldn't bitch about it.

About that time, there were footsteps coming up the hallway, and Ava stopped at Peggy's office door. "Hi, I need to speak with you, Carter."

Carter had hoped he'd get out of the state before having to deal with Ava. "Of course, but we'll have to make it quick. I'm planning a trip to New York City." He watched as her face fell into a harsh expression.

"What's in New York City?" She folded her arms as if making an accusation.

"NYPD. They've asked me to come and help with a case." He wasn't going to explain himself any further. What he did wasn't her business, and she had really lost her mind questioning him in front of Peggy.

"I see," she said, as he opened the door, and she stepped around Peggy's desk to join him without so much as giving the older woman a second look. Carter thought she should give the woman her proper respects, but apparently, there was no honor among church whores.

He shut the door behind her and offered her a seat. "What do you think you're doing, coming here during the day?"

"Business," she said. Ava had really grown bold. "Besides, if I were to drop in at night, as usual, you'd probably be busy with another woman."

His phone rang, and he looked at the screen, seeing that it was his wife. "I've got to take this. One second, please."

"Whatever," said Ava. "I'm not going anywhere." She crossed her legs and folded her arms across her chest. Carter couldn't help but notice that she had not dressed too scantily, nor had she showed her usual displays of affection.

"Hello, darling," he said to his wife, hoping to get rid of her.

"Carter, sweetie. It's so good to hear your voice. I've had such a breakthrough here, and well, I think I'm going to come home for the weekend and share it with you." Her voice was so syrupy that it gave him a headache.

"Home? But you still have a month left, precious. I think you should stay."

"But why? I miss you, and I want one night with my husband in our bed. Have you forgotten what Saturday is, Carter?" Her voice took on an even squealier tone.

He racked his brain trying to remember. Their anniversary was near Christmas, so it wasn't that. It wasn't her birthday or his. "I give up." He let out a long breath as Ava seemed to grow more and more impatient.

Adrian giggled through the phone. "I knew you'd forgotten about the anniversary of our first date. Remember, we went to that fancy restaurant, and you kissed me for the first time?"

He had known he had better move fast to secure her hand. Her father was about to try and hook her up with a doctor, and Carter wasn't about to let the opportunity slip him by. "Of course, I do, baby. I just wanted to see if you remembered." He gave a chuckle. "But I'm afraid you can't come. I'm going to help the police with a case, and I won't even be home. It's a very ugly situation, and it needs my immediate attention."

The disappointment followed with more of her irritating sounds. "Oh no, that's just horrible, honey. You be safe."

Ava cleared her throat and gave him a hard look. He wondered what kind of bug had crawled up her ass. She certainly wasn't acting like herself. "Look, Adrian. I have to go. I have a meeting, and I can't miss it." He hurried off the phone with her, and Ava huffed and shook her head as he put down his phone.

"I should have expected the worst from you, being a married man and all."

"You certainly weren't deceived in any way, Ava. Now, what's the matter with you?"

"There's a rumor that you're fucking around with that slut Keely."

"You're not going to listen to idle gossip, are you?" Inside, one word played over and over in his head: *Fuck. Fuck. Fuck.*

"I need a job. I told you a month ago I needed to find employment soon, and my company finally laid me off for good this time. I need a job, and you're going to get me one."

"A job? What do you want to do, be a housekeeper? You could wear a sexy little maid's uniform." The things she wanted, he couldn't just give her. He was the pastor of the church but not the boss, even if they did put up with a lot of his shit.

"I want the assistant secretarial position."

He had to appreciate the fact that she wasn't extorting him for money, but the request just wasn't something he could do for her. "That position was permanently terminated years ago when the last girl left. Peggy handles things nicely, and we're a tight-running ship."

"I think you're going to have to make sure the position is open and ready for me to take it on. I've more than earned it by keeping my mouth shut, but if you fail to cooperate, I'll just have to tell everyone in the congregation how you manipulated me and forced me to have sex with you."

"Laying back and spreading your legs isn't forced sex, Ava. You might want to rethink your tactics a bit."

"Fuck you. I don't have to rethink anything. I'm serious. I've come in here and fucked you, sucked you off, and even waited on you hand and foot when your simpleton wife wouldn't do it. I'm tired of being underappreciated, and before I lose everything, I want you to make sure I'm taken care of."

Carter felt as if she needed to be reminded of who she was. "You're never going to get the job, Ava. Why would the church give it to a junkie whore like you? I mean, if I hadn't taken a special liking to you in the first place, you'd still be in some gutter, burping semen and smoking rocks."

Her face paled. "God washed away my sin, remember? Nothing you can say will hurt me. But I could hurt you. This junkie whore has nothing to lose, but you do."

"I can't give you a job, but maybe I can get you some money. Would that be cool?"

"It will buy you some time. That's for sure." Her eyes narrowed, all the adoration she had for him once was gone.

"It hurts me that you find it so necessary to try and come against me, Ava." He shook his head. "I really thought you cared more for the church than this."

"It has nothing to do with the church and everything to do with you."

"But it does hurt the church, Ava. We're strapped. The elders are already struggling, so I doubt they'll add another position to the staff."

She closed her eyes tightly, and tears leaked down her cheeks. "I was supposed to be the only one, Carter. It's bad enough you made me share you with your stupid wife, but now some slut too?" She got up from the chair and walked to the door that led to the hallway. Carter wondered if she didn't want to look into the other woman's eyes on the way out. "I've got more pride than that, and it's time I start to focus on me. I need rent money. I need a new car. All of these things, you'll make sure I have them, or I'll tell everyone all about you and me." She hurried to the door as he sat there stunned by her audacity.

CHAPTER 11

DAREK

"I'm fine," said Lizzy as she paced Darek's living room. "There's no need to worry about me, and I'm not going to take the rest of the day off." She had agreed to go to his house and cool down from her latest outburst before lunch, but Darek still wanted to know what had triggered her temper.

"I know you said you're fine a hundred times, baby, but that doesn't tell me anything about why it happened." He looked up at her from the couch where she had been sitting not a minute earlier.

She stopped in front of him. "So much for you being smart enough to leave well enough alone," she said softly but not quite under her breath.

He tried not to be offended. "Hey, I want to know if someone hurt you. I understand if it's a touchy subject, but you obviously have some issues you need to deal with. Maybe you should talk to someone about it."

"A shrink? Seriously?" She shook her head, her anger quickly escalating.

But he wasn't about to back down. "Was there something more to the relationship with Robert that you haven't told me about?"

Her jaw fell slack as she closed her eyes as if to collect herself.

"Jesus, no!" she finally said. "That man was gold; he was everything to me. He treated me like a father *should* treat their children, and he never laid a finger on me." She pointed, poking his chest. "I don't want to talk about it."

"Fine," said Darek. He reached out, grabbed her wrist, and pulled her close. "I care about you, okay? I care, and if you need to talk to anyone and you don't want to see a shrink, you can tell me anything, Lizzy. Okay?" He searched her eyes, but all he found were more storm clouds.

"Let's change the subject. Please." She gave him a sharp look.

"Fine, yes, by all means." He took a deep cleansing breath and blew it out. "We can look on the bright side of things. We got Antonio to confess, and the asshole will be spending a long fucking time behind bars."

"It was even easier than I thought it would be. We're going to have more and more nuts like him coming out of the woodwork if we don't figure out who this killer is and bring him in soon." She wrapped her arms around her middle as she sat beside him.

"People like him are always going to be out there. Ken really stirred the shit pot when he said there were others out there doing his bidding. No telling how many are plotting to be his copycats."

"I don't want to think about maybes. I want to think about what is. The killer hasn't really made a move in a while that we know of. So, we have to assume that the next victim might fall in our lap at any moment."

"He's overdue."

"Or maybe the killer is dead or already locked up on another charge." She shrugged.

"So, in the meantime, you should take it easy, and I'll keep working on Sin's mind."

Lizzy turned to face him as he eased back and angled toward her. "Did you ever hear any more about New Orleans?" she asked.

Darek had, but he couldn't tell her. "No, and I don't want you worrying yourself over that. I'm handling it. It was just a stupid drive-by gang initiation like you said. Nothing more." He wanted her to keep believing that as long as possible, and there shouldn't be a reason for that to ever change.

"All of this taking a break shit is really getting on my nerves, Darek. Could you please stop acting like my father and start acting like my boyfriend again?"

"That's easy enough." He leaned in and brought his mouth down on hers. They kissed each other deeply and languidly, letting their bodies relax into one another.

She pulled away as his stomach growled. "Wow, you sound like you're smuggling a grizzly bear in there. We should go out and get something to eat on our way back to the office."

"I agree. Because if I stay here any longer, I'm going to have you in bed, and we'll both be in hiding for the rest of the day."

"That's the only way I'd consider taking the day off."

Darek shook his head at the stubborn girl. "You can pick the spot, and after we eat, I'll take you to the office so you can finish up working up the report while I go and make arrangements for Sin."

Lizzy got to her feet and pulled his arm, encouraging him to stand up with her. "I see how it is. You're going to keep me busy writing up reports while you're out investigating Sin."

"That's what Reed wanted."

"I can't believe you two are ganging up on me." She leaned in and kissed him, a quick soft peck on the cheek.

"He wanted me to show him what I'm made of, so I'm calling in a person who reached out to me and told me that Sin was once a member of his church. Carter Hamilton."

The name caught her attention like he figured it would. "The preacher from TV?"

"The one and only," he said, smiling because she seemed impressed.

"He just reached out? Just like that? It's kind of a coincidence." She gave him a sideward glance like she wasn't buying it.

"I might have put some feelers out, and he responded." Darek didn't want to tell her too much about how he got in touch because he hated lying to Lizzy. In a perfect world, she'd be his true partner in crime, knowing all of his darkest secrets and being his right-hand girl, but that was never going to be possible, with Lizzy or any woman. Raven was the only one who had come close to being that for him.

As he took Lizzy's hand and led her to the door where they slipped on their shoes, he realized that he hadn't thought of Raven in quite a bit. He felt a pang of uncertainty and guilt but shook it off. When the going got tough, Raven bailed. He wasn't sure he'd ever forgiven her for that, even though he'd known it was for the best and in a small way, he'd wanted her to go. Relationships could be so confusing, and right or wrong, he'd formed one with her.

"Are you okay?"

He turned and saw the way she looked at him like she wasn't sure he was still with her. "Yeah, sorry. I'm just a little distracted." He opened the door for her, and they made it all the way into the car before she attempted a guess.

"Is it about your phone call?" she asked. She'd stayed in the living room while he'd gone to the bathroom to talk to Carter.

He hadn't told her much about it, but it had been on his mind. "No, that was nothing. Just a checkup about my mother."

"How's she doing?"

"Good." He gave a nod and got them on the road headed back to the office.

He would have to find out if Carter had confided to Sin about more than he had confessed. It was highly possible that Ken's influences were built around everything that Carter had told him. He couldn't imagine someone sitting around plotting something so big and not having someone there to influence him, and while Ken Sin was no Bay Collins, Darek wouldn't be surprised if Carter hadn't been so enamored by Ken's fame, no matter how diluted, that he bragged about a lot of things he shouldn't have with the man.

With any luck, he and Bay would be able to get to the bottom of it when they met. He needed to call Bay and tell him Carter was on his way. Maybe Bay would have some questions of his own; he could let The Slayer slay him with questions.

"You could let me help you, you know? I'm not afraid to go back in and interrogate Sin again." Lizzy squared her shoulders as she shifted in her seat beside him.

"Reed would have my balls if I let you anywhere near him." He knew better. "I'm not jeopardizing my career to let you prove a point. You heard him. He wants me to prove myself, and maybe if I do good with this, then Reed will hire me."

"Fine. I don't want to ruin that for you." She leaned closer to the window, staring out at the traffic.

"You could never ruin anything," he said, reaching over to take her hand. He brought it to his lips and thought about how thankful he was for second chances.

CHAPTER 12

BAY

Bay stepped out of his private elevator and into the lobby in front of his office as Mia rushed ahead of him to get the door unlocked. "Stop doting over me," he said as she held the door open for him. "You didn't care this much before you ran away. There's no bother trying to make up for it now." They had already had a busy day, and it was only ten o'clock. But Bay had been for his checkup and learned that his shoulder was healing nicely, and he wouldn't have to do any more physical therapy, which he hated.

"I *do* care, and being away has made me realize how much. I'm lost without you, Bay." Mia's voice was soft, and she kept her eyes on the floor most of the time.

"Will you stop? Please. I just want my bratty little girl back. I hate the whiny shit. If I wanted that, I'll call your sister to come back home." He liked Mia better when she had a hint of mischief in her eyes. He reached into this desk and took out a pad and pen. "Here."

Her eyes lit up, and she took a seat in the chair across from his desk. "You want me to take notes for you like a real secretary?"

"Not necessarily. I thought you should write a list of the places you want to go, the things you want to buy. I'm not prepared to let you out of my sight in the city just yet, but I'll take you shopping later on tonight if you like."

"You want to go shopping with me?" she asked with a hint of shock in her tone.

He'd never gone with her when she was on one of her mad spending sprees. "Yes. I suppose I could. I'd like a new suit, and maybe you could help me choose a color."

"That might be fun." She readied the pen at the paper. "What is my limit?"

"If you promise to stop looking like it's the end of the world, you could spend as much as you like."

As soon as the words hit her ears, Bay saw the gleam he loved so much twinkle in her eyes. "I want a car. Can I have a car?"

He shook his head. "Mia, you don't even have your license."

"I want my license then. But could I? I've always wanted a car of my very own."

Bay shook his head. "I don't feel safe about it, but maybe for your next birthday. If you take a driving course."

She slumped a bit, her posture and pout just how he liked it. "Fine." She looked away, rolling her eyes before she put the pen to work.

"That's my girl. I've missed your spirit, Mia. Don't ever lose that."

"Will you be taking me out for lunch?" She uncrossed her legs and moved her hand down to her thigh to toy with the hem of her skirt. Bay knew her appetite had changed during her time with Max Smith, and around noon, she was bound to have an itch.

"Yes. You can even pick the restaurant. Maybe we'll have a little fun before." Bay liked it when she was happy, and it was a hell of a lot easier to make her that way than her sister.

His phone rang, and he glanced down to see that Lane Simon was calling. "Shit. I have to take this, Mia." He answered and kicked back in his chair, spinning it toward the window.

"How's it going, Lane?"

"Pretty good. Contractors are just about done with the remodel. The new windows look great, and I finally got the blood stains off the sidewalk."

Bay had thought the repairs would take much longer and the stains would never come out. "Sounds like things are looking good then."

"How are you feeling?" asked Lane. "Is the arm better?"

"Yes, it's good. I went for an appointment this morning. One of those follow-up deals."

"Good deal, man. Look, I've been contacted about Justin Finch. Were you aware that he died?"

Bay realized he hadn't called him. "Shit. I meant to call you, Lane, but things have been so busy."

Lane chuckled. "No worries, Bay. I get it. It's just that I was in charge of his will, and since you've taken on all of my old workloads, it's up to you to meet with his beneficiary and make sure that everything is set."

"Who is the beneficiary?"

"Brandy. She gets it all."

"Wait, you're saying that Corey's Brandy gets all of Justin's money? He didn't leave it to family or anyone else?"

"Nope, just her," Lane said. "When he made the will a year ago, she was the only person in his life."

"I wonder if she knew that before he died." Bay had a feeling that little miss Brandy might have had Justin killed in order to have both Corey and Justin's money. Both men were extremely loaded.

He must have leaned on Brandy when the Betty relationship fell apart. He smiled, knowing that this was an opportunity he hadn't expected.

Bay thought of one of the last times he talked to Justin. When the man had said he needed help with a marriage license. Bay had accommodated him at the time, thinking he had everything under control with Brandy and Corey's fortune. Bay had helped him and simply put the information in his back pocket for a rainy day. He hadn't expected it to pour so soon.

"I know it's a lot to burden you with, man. I bet your caseload is a bitch after being shot, but I can't deal with it. There's no way I can leave the restaurant, and you're going to need her to sign a few things and produce a death certificate. After that, it should be filed in her county."

"No, it's not a problem. I'll take care of it."

"I can't believe what happened," Lane said. "I talked to the police, and they said that Justin tried to defend himself, but in the confusion, he'd grabbed a gun that wasn't even loaded."

"That's a bit surprising, isn't it?" Bay didn't think that sounded like the Justin he knew at all. The man would know if his gun was loaded or not. And why would he even have a gun around the house that wasn't loaded and ready to use? Something was off.

"I thought so, but you never know. Anything is possible. I mean, if Brandy can pull a Rambo move out of her ass like shooting the three suspects with an AK, then I guess we shouldn't be so shocked."

"You know, Lane, a professor of ours once told me that when one thing doesn't make sense, it's a coincidence, but when two things don't, it's usually deliberate."

"Sounds like something The Grifter would say."

"That's exactly who said it. I've always thought it made a lot of sense. I don't trust coincidence." He never had.

"So, when you say that, what you're really saying is, you think that someone unloaded his gun and plotted his death?" His voice came through the phone with an amused tone.

"It's not impossible. But I can promise you this, if there was something fishy going on, I'm going to get to the bottom of it when I get there."

"Oh, that reminds me. Weren't you an original investor in his second store?"

Bay sat up straight in his chair. "As a matter of fact, yes, I was. Seth Stone had invested as well."

"Well, with Seth dead, that just leaves you and me."

"He paid off his debt."

"That he did, but there was a clause in the loan forms. I drew them up myself. Maybe you should take a look at them. You've just inherited two sporting good stores or at least a part of them."

"How?"

"I had it written in that if we helped him out, in the event of his death, we'd take ownership. He was supposed to tell you all about it. They would revert back to him after he paid us back, and then we'd still own a ten percent share if he passed away. When he finished paying us off, he seems to have forgotten to file it. It was in the contract you signed, Bay. Don't tell me you didn't read it."

He vaguely remembered. "Does Brandy know that?"

"I imagine you'll be the one to tell her. She seemed like a good girl, though. I'm sure you won't have any problems with her."

That was the way she had come off, like a good girl, but Bay had to questions her All-American Sunshine act. She might be beautiful and blond, but so was he, and he wouldn't trust himself if he were anyone else.

Not only did she fake her marriage with Corey, and was no doubt collecting a nice windfall from him, but now Justin was leaving her his money too. She had to be good for tens of millions. There was no way he'd let her take it all without sharing.

"I'm sure I can handle her."

"I'm sure you can," said Lane. "But call me if you need anything. I know these things can be a pain in the ass if you don't deal with them all the time and when so much emotion is involved. I'm sure she's a real mess after losing two men she cared about so soon after each other."

"I'll keep that in mind, but I'm sure I'll be fine. It might be nice to get away for a day or two." He looked across the room at Mia whose head came up when he mentioned going away.

He wasn't sure what he'd have to do with her, but he didn't think it would be a good idea for her to go along.

After a friendly farewell, he got off the phone and walked across the room to his file cabinet. The deal he'd made with Justin all those years ago over the second store was recorded somewhere. He had always kept a folder of personal documents, and when he found it, he took it to the desk.

Mia walked over to join him, taking a spot on his knee. "Here's my list." She had a list with about twenty things on it and passed the paper to Bay, who quickly skimmed through to the bottom.

"Five of these are shoes." She had a closet full of fucking shoes, but if she wanted more, that was what she'd get.

She gave him a clever grin. "I'm a shoe whore; I can't help it."

"You'll have to be a much different kind of whore to get the rest of these things." Her list consisted of mostly lingerie and sex toys. "I approve."

Her smile beamed, and she stretched out her neck to kiss him. "I thought that we might have some fun."

"You know we will." He gave her a pop on the bottom, and she giggled.

But then she sighed and reached up to stroke his hair. "Will I be going with you when you go away?"

He closed his eyes, loving the feel of her fingers caressing his scalp. "I'm not sure. I'll think about it, but it's work-related, and it's going to be something I don't do a lot of. I shouldn't bring any distractions along for the ride." She was always his favorite distraction.

"Think about it? I'll be on my best behavior." She reached down and stroked his cock through his pants.

He hissed in a breath and looked into her eyes. "Hm, you really do fall right back into it, don't you?" He patted her bottom and then kissed her cheek. "Why don't you show me what you've missed most of all?"

Without another word, she slipped down between his legs as he eased back in his chair. He knew right then how much he'd really missed her.

CHAPTER 13

CARTER

It wasn't bad enough that he had to waste an entire trip to New York City meeting up with Darek and Ken fucking Sin, but he'd had to get there flying coach for the first time in ages. He hadn't realized how spoiled to the better things he'd become until he had to eat stale honey-roasted peanuts while the woman next to him picked her toenails.

All of the shitty looks in the world hadn't deterred her picking her talons, and he'd finally told the woman just what he thought of her disgusting habit. *Nervous picker?* Was that even a thing?

He had made it to his hotel room by the end of the day, and when he called Darek, he told him the name of the restaurant he wanted to meet him at. He knew Bakes was owned by Bay Collins but hadn't thought the man would be joining them until he walked in and saw the platinum head of his like a beacon at a back table.

Darek wasn't there yet, but he was sure it wasn't a coincidence. He walked over to the table, and Bay stood, shaking his hand. "Did you have a good flight?"

Carter frowned. It was just like Bay to know which buttons to push. He had long believed the guy to be psychic. He pulled up a chair and sat across from him. "It was okay. I thought Darek would beat me here."

"You know how it is, busy detective, always on the case. He's probably still trying to figure out who put out that hit on us."

"Yeah, I bet. How are you doing?" He gestured to Bay's wounded arm. He'd expected Bay to still be wearing a sling, but he seemed to be doing well.

"It's good. I was lucky not to need a lot of therapy, and I didn't lose the mobility they first expected."

He may not have lost a lot of mobility, but Carter could definitely tell that Bay favored his other arm much more. Was it a habit from the healing process, or was the man full of shit? Bay was just the type to play off an injury. He liked to think of himself as a god, totally untouchable.

"That's wonderful news, friend. I've been praying for your fast recovery." Bay lifted his glass to his lips and took a long pull as whiskey was placed in front of Carter. "Thank you," he said as he took a long look at the waitress's ass as she walked away. "She's nice. Did you hire her?"

"No, I leave that fun to other people, but I have met her and could get you her number if you like. Or maybe have her drop by your hotel. I'm sure there's not anything she wouldn't do for me."

"Let me see how her service is, and I just might take you up on that offer."

"The wife still away on the mission?" Bay's brows rose.

Carter didn't want to even think about Adrian. "Yes, and I dodged a bullet coming here. She was about to hop the next plane home."

"So, how are things back home? With the church? Is your congregation still in love with you?"

"Are you asking if they'd have any reason to want me dead? The answer is no. I don't believe anyone would try to take me out. The shooting had nothing to do with me."

Bay's attention turned to something behind him, and he glanced around to see Darek had finally made it.

The two men stood and greeted him. "I hope someone died," said

Bay. "Otherwise, you couldn't possibly have a good excuse for making me wait."

"Sorry, I couldn't get away from the office. Lizzy wanted to know all about the meeting with Sin, when we're going, what I will say and have Carter say and so forth."

"While you mention it," said Carter, taking his seat. "What do you want me to say to him? Is there anything in particular we'll explore?"

"Darek tells me you have a rather strange past with Ken Sin."

Carter already knew what Bay wanted to know and where the questions were leading. "Yes, I knew him quite well, better than I let on before. I was nervous that you'd all think I told him about Virginia, but I swear to you on the good book that I did not tell him anything that would make him come after us."

"I guess it could all be much worse, then," said Bay, still not looking impressed.

Darek shrugged. "Well, I think if Ken knew I was involved, he'd have already blown my cover."

"You're right about that," said Bay. "Make sure that you don't let anyone, not even Sin, know that you two are old friends." He directed the comment to Carter, who only slightly felt offended for being singled out.

"I wasn't expecting you to be here, Bay," he said, giving Darek a pointed look.

"Come on now; you didn't think I was going to let you get away with not seeing me while you were in town. Besides, I've come to offer hospitality to an otherwise boring visit."

He looked around at the restaurant. "I must say, this is a nice place."

Bay raked his hand through his hair. "Thank you." The waitress walked up and brought Darek a drink, and then Bay leaned over. "Bring us each a steak, medium rare, and put a rush on them please."

The girl was practically fucking him with her eyes, and Carter smiled, knowing that Bay wanted him to be envious of the attention. "Yes, Mr. Collins." She turned and sauntered away with a bit more spring in her step.

"Thank you," said Darek, putting down the menu.

"Well, it's the least I can do. It's not often our friend leaves his sanctuary to come to hang with us common sinners."

Darek smiled but took another drink as Carter sat back in his chair, hoping to look unaffected by Bay's tone. "I thought I just might go by your other establishment for a bit of adult fun while I'm in town. I'm on a bit of a solo journey this time, lucky for me." The last time he'd come to town had been with his wife, and she was so buttoned-up and proper, she'd faint dead away at the thought of fucking her husband in front of a mirror, much less seeing another couple fuck right in front of her.

"You're welcome anytime. I'll call and make sure that your VIP band is waiting for you. I myself will be out of town."

"Where does excitement take you now, Bay?" Darek's eyes narrowed. "Don't tell me you're going to see your wife."

"No. I wanted to tell you, but I thought I might let you both in on the fun. I only just got a call from Lane earlier today."

"You're going to see Lane?" asked Carter, wondering if it had anything to do with the shooting.

Bay smiled. "No, I'm going to Justin's house in Michigan. When Lane quit the practice, he gave me all of his cases and legal responsibilities. He said that Justin got with him some time ago and made a will. I'm going to go and make sure it's all being handled properly, and it's not really something I can do over the phone."

"You're going to stay at Justin's house?" Darek leaned forward in his chair. "Maybe you could look into Betty?"

Bay shook his head. "No, but I'm sure I'll have time to dig around. I will try to find something."

Carter needed to get a word in and put his hand flat on the table in front of them. "Wait, he had a will?"

"Yeah, he did. With all of that money, it's no wonder. I just don't know why he left it all to Brandy Walker."

Carter's head whipped up so fast that he could have sworn he heard the snap of a whip. "Brandy? As in Corey's girlfriend?"

Darek narrowed his eyes. "Why would he do that?"

"Then who is this Betty person? His mother?" The last thing Carter needed was another heir gumming up the works of his plan.

"She's his online girlfriend, and the person we think is the real killer," Darek said.

"It's a long story," said Bay. "I'll tell you about it later."

"Why Brandy?" Carter didn't know what was so special about the girl.

Bay shrugged. "I guess they were pretty close. He left her everything apparently. Not a soul other than her to divide it with."

Carter's head was swimming with emotions. Not only did he have a little anger, thinking that the bitch must have had something to do with Justin's death, but she was also going to get a fuck ton of money, and his bargain with her was about to be renegotiated. He had told her half, and he meant half of all. He'd be sure to let her know.

"She's going to need a lot of prayers for wisdom," Carter said. "You know, I've always wanted to see Justin's house. I heard he built most of it himself and refused to use power tools. He was quite proud of it. I wonder if she'll be selling it or not. I know I'd like to check it out and see if it's something I might be interested in. Would you mind if I come along? I'd like to offer my condolences as well."

Bay smiled. "I think that would be great. I could use the traveling companion, and you can listen to my confessions and tell me if I'm going to Hell or not."

"You'd think that was clear already," said Darek.

Bay gave a sly smile. "Well, maybe you can save my soul then. Make a better man out of me."

"Then it's all set," Carter said. "When do we leave?"

"Late tomorrow, when you're done with your Sin ordeal. We'll be making a road trip out of it and get a jump start on the weekend. Hopefully, we'll be able to make it back home in time for a new week."

"That sounds good to me. I'm ready to get this meeting with Sin behind, but I think I'll unwind at the club a little tonight, loosen up a bit."

Darek gave him a scolding look. "Just don't get too relaxed. I need you to show up."

"I'll be in the crow's nest with Mia," said Bay.

Darek eased back off the table. "How's she doing?"

"She's conflicted," said Bay. "I thought things might go back to the way they were before, but when I took her out shopping earlier, she was a mess."

"You went shopping?" Carter couldn't imagine Bay holding a shopping bag, much less going into a store on his own. "I figured you had personal shoppers."

"No, that's reserved for televangelists." He gave Carter a wink.

"I wish. My church's finances are tied up right now, and they canceled my lease on the private plane."

"Damn, that's harsh," said Darek. He and Bay exchanged an amused look.

"If I see you later, I'll say hi." Bay took a sip of his bourbon.

Carter liked being with the top man in charge everywhere he went. "Maybe you can introduce me to the dirtiest girl around."

"No, I'm sorry. I'm afraid Darek's already run her off."

Darek looked up, giving Bay a harsh expression.

"Wait, you were at the club?" Carter chuckled.

"You should have seen the woman he was with. She was a Zodiac favorite. A real hellcat from what I remember."

"That's enough," said Darek. He turned his attention to Carter. "It's over with us, and I'm already seeing someone else."

Carter knew better than to give Darek a hard time. The detective had no sense of humor. Bay wasn't much better. Carter hoped that he and Bay would get along on the road. He wanted to meet with Brandy face to face and tell her that he was onto her newfound fortune and that he wanted half of that too. The only thing he had to worry about was Bay. He doubted that the man even realized that Justin had planned for Brandy to get Corey's money as well.

The conversation fell as their food came, and Carter noticed the strange vibe in the air between Bay and Darek. The two had exchanged looks several times, and he was sure that they both had their reservations about him.

Once he had the money he needed, he'd be able to take care of his business and then some. With Ava wanting the job and on the verge of making a stink, as well as Keely's threats, he had to be careful. Things could only get worse if he didn't nip their threats in the bud.

Once he had all of that money, not only would he pay off the two women, but he was planning to keep his nose clean for a while and his dick in his pants. He didn't need the drama that the woman always seemed to bring. He understood why his father had found Peggy, a woman to fuck who would be discreet with his indiscretions. He thought he'd found that with Ava, but now she was in a desperate situation and only making it worse for the both of them.

Twenty minutes later, the conversation had come full circle, and he finished his steak. As Bay paid the check, Carter got to his feet. "It was good to see you guys, but I'm afraid I need to get back to the hotel and get some sleep for my big meeting tomorrow." He gave Darek a smile. "What time should I expect you?"

"I'll pick you up at eight. That will give them time to have Sin ready."

"Sounds good, my friend. Thanks again, Bay. I look forward to our trip." He looked forward mostly to getting his hands on Justin's money. He only hoped that Brandy wouldn't make trouble for them both.

CHAPTER 14

BAY

After Carter had left their little dinner party, Darek had warned Bay to keep an eye out for Carter at Taunt. So, he and Mia sat up in the crow's nest and watched the cameras as she sat sulking.

"Cheer up, or I'm going to make you gangbang that room of men." He pointed to a screen, and Mia sighed.

"I know better. You wouldn't let me have that much fun." She sank back in her seat and brought her knees up close to her chin.

Bay didn't understand her mood. He'd tried to make things back how they'd been, but when it came time to go shopping, she'd clammed up and gotten progressively more standoffish. "I thought I was going to give you some fun today. Why are you back to sulking?"

"I guess I'm just not content." She shook her head.

"I thought things were back to normal."

She gave a weary laugh. "That's the problem, Bay. I ran away from normal for a reason. I wanted all of those things you promised buying me, and for a moment, it was exciting, but then I realized it was just more of the same."

Bay turned his attention from the monitor to her with a pointed expression. "You're saying I'm dull? Predictable? I've never been accused of that before." He tried not to be offended. "Is it really so horrible being in love with me, Mia?"

She moved her chair closer and sank down beside him. "The only thing hard about it is knowing that this is all it's ever going to be."

"Poor little darling, always getting her way. How terrible it must be to have someone love you enough to give you your every fucking wish."

Mia's hand fell on his arm. "What did you say?"

Bay turned his eyes back to the monitor and realized what had slipped from his lips. He had used the *love* word with her.

"Do you love me?" she asked softly.

"Of course, you're my sister in law, my lover, my family. Why wouldn't I?"

"Do you think we could ever be more than what we are now?"

"Is there anything more? We're practically together every minute of the day, with Lila gone."

"Are you going to let me go on this trip with you?"

His back stiffened, and he hated to have to break the news to her. "I'm sorry, Mia. I already have a friend coming along. You remember Carter, don't you? The preacher who came to see me at the hospital. He's in town, and he's riding along to give his condolences to Brandy." Bay knew why he was really going, but she didn't need to know everything.

Her face twisted like she'd been kicked in the gut. "But what about me? Where am I supposed to go? You won't let me stay in the house alone, and I can't go back to my friend's. Her boyfriend moved in the day I left."

"You'll go spend some time with Lila. You two need to spend some time together. She probably needs you more than ever."

Mia looked outraged. "To wait on her hand and foot? To be her punching bag? No thanks."

"To be her sister, silly girl. And don't act like you don't need that too. All of this, you and me, and what we have? It will all be here, Mia. When you're ready to realize how good it is. Meanwhile, I refuse to entertain your sadness. If you feel cheated and bored, there's a whole kingdom downstairs, princess. Go and find some adventure."

"You'll be angry." She shook her head. "I don't really want anyone else, at least not without you in the mix."

He smiled. The loyal pet was too attached to her master. But then he remembered his words. He, in fact, was too attached to her.

Movement out of the corner of his eyes had him glancing at the front door monitor, and just as he realized it was Carter at the door, his business phone rang. He reached over and picked it up. "He's with me. I'll be down in a second." He hung up the phone and got to his feet. "My friend is here. Come along if you like."

He walked down the staircase that took him out of his nest and onto the main floor. Carter had already turned a few heads, despite his attempts to blend in. He had lost the perfect part of his hair and that helmet-like hairstyle. Couple that with the fact that he had let his facial hair grow in a bit, and you couldn't really tell he was Pastor Carter Hamilton.

"Well, aren't you blending in?" asked Bay. "I barely spotted you. If my man hadn't flagged you down and called me, I'd have missed you."

"Yeah, well, I'm used to sinners, but I don't want to counsel any tonight. Tonight, I want to be an enabler."

"Well, I can help with that." Bay took out his wristband and handed it to him. "This will get you anything you want and damned near anyone."

There was already a lot of attention on them. It wasn't often that Bay stood out on the floor, but when he did, he always had a crowd of hopefuls around him, especially when he was passing out VIP bands.

Carter put on the band, and by the time he looked up, there were already a crowd of desiring women around him and a few men.

Mia locked her arm with Bay's, and he kissed her cheek. "Mia and I will be upstairs if you need us."

He watched as Carter curled his finger at a woman who stood across the room. She was in her thirties and wore a dress that was cut all the way down the front, making it more like a robe. If it weren't for the belt, it would have been completely open.

"I want to stay down here," said Mia. "Can't we go to a voyeur room?"

"Do you want to watch?" asked Carter, his ego getting the better of him, in Bay's opinion.

"Could we?" She turned her eyes to Bay. "Please."

"I'm not sure that's a good idea, kitten. My friend might like his privacy." He had never considered watching the pastor get off, but he wanted to know why Mia was so eager.

"I'm not opposed to being watched, especially if this little thing gets off on it." He eyed Mia up and down, and she drew herself closer to Bay. "She's sure attached to you." He pulled his woman closer, and she leaned in and kissed his earlobe before whispering into his ear. "Deanna would like us all to follow her."

Bay looked over at Mia and shrugged. But the girl hurried behind the couple as the woman pulled Carter away and led them all to a room.

Once they were all inside, Bay shut the door behind them, and the two girls began kissing. Mia giggled, clearly enjoying herself. Bay wasn't sure if his friend knew what he was getting into, but he looked over and found Carter taking off his shirt.

Bay smiled and shook his head. "Come along, Mia. You've had your fun." He tried to get her to leave with him, but he wasn't going to beg. After asking twice, he turned to see Carter licking his lips as he watched the two women caress each other's breasts.

He decided that it wasn't for him, and instead of trying to pull Mia out of there, he leaned over and tapped Carter on the shoulder. "Have fun, man. I've got other guests to check on."

"Seriously?"

"Yeah, I'll see you tomorrow. Don't let yourself get too carried away."

Bay was out the door and halfway down the hall when he heard his name. "Bay!" He wasn't about to look back.

"I just thought we'd have some fun," Mia said. "I didn't think that you'd care. You've fucked Lila with your other friends. You told me you did."

"And you're not Lila. I'd give Lila to the highest bidder, Mia. But you? I'm not sharing you. You're either mine, or you're out. Plain and simple. You can use your time in the islands to figure out what you want. But I'm done."

"I'm sorry. I just thought you'd want me to be everything I can for you."

"You can be, Mia. That's all I want." He took to the stairs, and she followed.

"I just wanted to watch with you."

"I don't have that kind of control over all of my friends, baby. It's a power play. Carter is a different species. I have to make a different play when it comes to him." He opened the door, and they took a seat by the windows. "Look." He pointed to the threesome that was about to go down in the front room. "You've got a good view from right here."

"Bay?"

He took a deep breath. "What?"

"Do you really not want to share me?"

"It's my preference not to, Mia. You're my selfish thing. The one thing I have for myself, even though I'm not supposed to have you. I'll always be selfish with you."

"Because you love me?"

"Is that what you want to hear, Mia?"

"Lila says that you've barely said it to her. In all this time, even though she's carrying your child. She asked me if you'd said it to me. I kept insisting there was nothing to us, but I finally had to admit that no, you'd never said it.

"It's just words, Mia."

She shook her head. "They have meaning, Bay."

"Actions are better." He reached out and stroked her cheek. "I think my actions have spoken loud and clear in the past. You had me right where you wanted me when you left." It was all he could give her at the moment.

CHAPTER 15

DAREK

After a long night of making love with Lizzy, Darek finally dragged himself out of bed the next morning. As his eyes adjusted, he looked at the clock. "Shit, I'll never make it on time." He had the meeting all set up for eight-thirty, and there was no way he'd make it to the hotel to get Carter and then back. He would have to ask the man to meet him there, and even then, he'd be pressing his luck. To make things worse, he'd even asked Bay to make sure that Carter didn't overdo it at the club. But that was before he'd gotten the late-night booty call from his girl.

Lizzy was in the kitchen milling around, and while he couldn't see what she was up to, he could smell the bacon frying and the coffee brewing as the aroma wafted through the air and hit his nose.

He got out of bed and headed to the bathroom, slamming the door behind him. When he was done with this shower, Lizzy was waiting on the other side of the bathroom door.

"Hey, sleepyhead. I hope it was okay to let you sleep a little longer. You just looked so comfortable."

Darek threw his hands up in frustration. "No, it was the worst day to do that, trust me. I've got my meeting this morning, and I'm never going to make it across town to pick up Carter Hamilton."

"Oh no!" Lizzy looked horrified. "I'm so sorry, Darek. I feel like such an idiot. Do you need me to help with anything?"

Darek hurried to his closet, toweling off as he went. "No, it's okay. I'm just going to throw something on and speed across town. If I can't get him to meet me at the station, I'll go swing by and pick him up."

Lizzy hurried to the dresser and found him some underwear and socks. "I'm so sorry. I cooked breakfast and everything."

"I'll take something on the road, baby. Bacon and coffee will be perfect."

"I'll make it up to you later. I'll be at the office in a bit if you need me."

He wished that he could include her, but he knew Reed would be pissed if he did. He pulled his shorts and pants on and then quickly pulled a shirt over his head on the way to sit on his bed. Lizzy had left his socks there, and his boots were by the door.

She ran to the kitchen, and when he was on his way to the door, she handed him his breakfast and kissed his cheek. He hurried out to the car and stopped to give her another, longer kiss before getting into the car.

"Good luck. Let me know what you find out."

"I will. I'll see you at the office when I'm done." He got into the car and started it. Not wasting any time, he backed out and sped down the road. He had to get Carter on the phone and find out what to do. He took his phone out and dialed his number.

"Darek, are you on your way?" asked Carter.

"I'm just leaving the house. Is there any way you could take a cab?"

"I'm sure I can swing it."

"Thanks, man. My girlfriend thought she'd let me sleep in an extra half hour. I don't know what she was thinking."

Carter laughed. "I left my lady at the club. I tell you, that place comes in handy. I love the drama-free type. There needs to be more of those at my church."

"I hear you, man. I'll head on over to the prison and make sure that they have him ready." He really hated that his plans had gotten fucked up, but as long as everything else went okay and Reed didn't have to know about anything, he should be okay.

Luckily, Carter seemed upbeat, and Darek was glad the man had gotten laid. "I'll see you there," he said before ending the call.

Darek got onto the main road and didn't let off the gas until it was time to exit. He cruised into the prison parking lot and hurried into the building to check in. He made it just in time and wouldn't have to make any excuses if Reed managed to check up on him. Now all he had to do was wait on Carter.

When Carter arrived fifteen minutes later, they still hadn't brought Ken Sin down to the room. Darek walked up to the desk. "Hey, I'm Detective Darek Blake. I have a meeting with an inmate, and they haven't called me back yet."

The woman gave him a blank stare. "Okay, I'll see what the problem is." She got up from her desk and spoke with another lady, who walked over.

"Did you have his interview scheduled?" the new woman asked.

Darek nodded. "Yes, and I assumed that they'd call me by now."

About that time, a man walked in and whispered something in the other woman's ear. They exchanged a look, and the man approached Darek. "There's a lockdown on that block, which means we can't let anyone in or out, scheduled meetings or not."

"You're kidding me." He had everything sorted and now this? "What time do you think we'll be able to see him?" He didn't want to wait all day. "I'm the detective working on his case, so I'd appreciate you finding out what you can."

"Okay, let me go check and see how long they'll be." The man walked away, and Darek returned to where Carter waited patiently in the lobby.

"Did you find out anything?" he asked, looking at his gold watch.

"Nothing about Sin, but they had a lockdown in his block, so it could be a little while." Darek wondered if there was a fight or if someone had gotten killed. He knew those lockdowns could take hours, no matter the situation, and he was going to have to call Reed and see if he could help push things along if something didn't happen soon.

Carter tugged at his collar. "I swear this place is burning up."

"Yeah, and it doesn't smell that great either." Darek wasn't happy about waiting.

"I was just about to say," said Carter. "It doesn't help that I'm nervous. I never got a chance to finish telling you about him. I didn't want to get too into it with Bay there. I could already feel the tension between us. I felt like the two of you were feeling me out or something."

Darek wasn't going to lie. "Well, in all honesty, we were. We're not one hundred percent sure about this hit. We know it wasn't us, and while I hate to accuse anyone of being involved, you are a pretty big deal. Someone could have been after you, thought you'd be there."

"I'd think Lane or Bay would have all of the enemies. Ethan and I being celebrities of sorts doesn't make us a bigger target than someone who puts people in jail for a living. And let's face it. You three have all affected other people's freedoms." He let out a long breath. "What I'm saying is, it could have very well been one of you they were after."

"Fair enough." Darek angled in his seat toward him. "So, tell me what you didn't want Bay to know. It seems we've got some time here. You said on the phone that he mentioned wanting what you had. What did you mean by that? The church followers, the fame?" Darek couldn't imagine someone as wild and scary as Ken Sin getting followers to take him seriously, but then again, the world was full of crazy people, all looking for something to believe in.

"He called me a cultist. Said that I had my people right where I wanted them. He asked me lots of questions about that, like he was obsessed with it. He even said he wanted to form his own following and have what I had." Carter closed his eyes and shook his head. "Maybe he tried to do that. Maybe it was all talk that led him here. But what I know is, I tried to explain to him it wasn't that easy. I told him that people like me, we can't abuse our power."

Darek couldn't help but give him an accusing look.

Carter held up his hands as if to make a point. "Sure, I do in ways. I'm not saying I'm perfect or the shining example I could be. But the people have to matter too. You have to care for them, listen to them, nurture them, feed them. If you don't, it all falls apart. But he said he could do it without all the work. I told him it was impossible."

"That's why he only claimed to have a following," said Darek. "That's what he hoped to accomplish. I think he hoped by admitting he was the killer and taking the credit, it would make for less work. But he didn't think it through." Darek knew Ken wasn't the murderer, but he had to know if Carter felt like he was capable of murder. Had locking him up been a service in any way? He knew the man had a violent streak, but just how far would he take it? "Do you think he's able to kill anyone?"

"I've seen his temper," said Carter. "But it was all small things. He once got angry at a woman at church who parked where he liked to park. She was an expecting mother, and he said that he should do her husband a favor and kick her in the stomach. I was appalled, of course. My wife was very upset over it, and I had to call him into my office over that. The family left our church, and it wasn't long after that when he left as well."

"The guy is a sicko." Darek let out a long breath, and before the two could continue their conversation, an officer walked over and joined them.

"Are you Officer Blake?"

"Detective Blake, yes. Have you been able to get our suspect to the visitation room yet?"

The man's expression fell. "I've been asked to bring you upstairs to the block."

Darek got to his feet. "Could Pastor Hamilton come along as well? He is here to counsel the inmate."

"I'll take you upstairs, and you can find out there. The block is on lockdown still, but—well, you'll see."

Darek shook his head. He had a feeling the guard had been asked not to say anything, and he was growing increasingly curious about the issue. "Come on, Carter. Let's go and see if we can get this interview over with."

On the way, it crossed his mind that whatever the lockdown was about, it might have concerned Sin. When they got upstairs and there were several guards standing in the narrow pass near the block entrance, Darek could tell that it was bad news.

"Detective Blake?"

"Yes, and this is Pastor Hamilton."

"I recognize you, Pastor. My wife watches your Sunday service every week."

"Thank you," said Carter. "Send her my best."

The man nodded, and though he seemed pleased to meet Carter, whatever was going on had him upset. "I'm Officer Crane," said the man as he led them past the other guards and into the block, where every cell was locked down and all the inmates were made to stand against the back wall of their cells, facing away. "I heard you were here and saw where you had an appointment with Kenny. I'm afraid that there's been a horrible occurrence. When the guards came through this morning, they found him. He appears to have hanged himself this morning after the first check."

Darek walked into the cell and found Sin on the floor. He had been cut down, part of his clothing still attached to his bunk. He'd cut the legs of his pants up and made an effective noose.

"He took his time to make the rope, probably plotted all night. When they did first check, he was reportedly still in his bed."

Carter peeked into the room and turned a ghostly white. "Dear Jesus," he mumbled.

Darek thought the same thing. With Sin dead, there was no more scapegoat.

They finished up with the guards, and when they finally got to leave, Darek walked Carter back out to the car. "I'll take you back to the hotel now. I know you're leaving, and I need to let my partner know about Sin." He unlocked the door, and the two got inside.

"Yeah, I think Bay will want to get on the road as soon as possible. I'll tell him about Sin. I'm sure he'll be glad the asshole's dead."

Darek shook his head, starting the car. "It's not a good thing. Believe me."

"What do you mean?"

"If someone else is murdered, this case is going wide open again, and it's not exactly been a cakewalk keeping my partner off of her theories, some of which have taken us dangerously close to having our secrets found out."

"Jesus, you really have been on the spot all this time, haven't you?"

Carters words were such an understatement they were nearly comical. "You have no idea. But don't worry. I'm going to do all I can to find out who is responsible. With any luck, the killer is going to get sloppy. And with Bay getting access to Justin's house and hopefully some of his records, we just might be able to find this killer before they kill again."

"It hasn't escaped me that my name is next on the list."

"Which is why you need to be careful." He gave Carter a pat on the back and then backed out of the space and headed to the hotel.

CHAPTER 16

CARTER

After the long morning, Carter returned to his room, not sure how to feel about Ken Sin's demise. He had known the man, hung out with him, and anytime anyone died, he always felt like it was such a waste, no matter how much of a piece of shit the person was.

Those thoughts always led to his father, and while some would argue that he wasn't a piece of shit, Carter knew better. He'd always known the man behind the curtain that everyone else couldn't see, the one that most ignored or made excuses for.

The best thing he'd learned from the man was how to manipulate people, how to play on their faults and make them feel like they were special, only so they'd open up.

He'd also learned that from one other person.

Carter remembered the first time he laid eyes on Bay Collins. The boy looked like a creature from heaven with his wild platinum hair and tanned skin, silver, and gold like he'd been brought to earth by divinity or perhaps a spaceship. But that wasn't all that was fascinating about the kid.

The other kids listened to him. He could speak in ways that held their attention. He both lifted them up and scolded them all in one sentence. He made Carter think, opened up his mind.

He'd only seen one other man manage to do such a thing, and to him, Carter was nothing but a sinner. Someone who could do no right, who God would punish for everything he thought and all of his wicked ways, and that was the difference between the two. While his father would knock him down for his sins, Bay accepted them.

He had watched Bay with his club for weeks and tried to be everywhere they were, always standing just outside of their circle, hoping for a way in.

One day, opportunity came when one boy nearly drowned in the lake. After that, the counselors had everyone split into groups of two, and the buddy system went into full effect.

"Pair off," said Tits. "This is going to be your new swim buddy. You don't go into the water unless you have your friend with you."

The kids started to split up, all choosing their partners, and Carter waited, knowing that Bay's group of friends were going to be a man short.

"Seth and Ethan. Corey and Justin." Bay pointed to the boys, and they paired off. Then he looked at Logan and Finn. "That leaves you two."

"I'll be your partner Bay," said Finn with an anxious look in his eye.

Bay shook his head and gave the boy a hard look. "You can't leave your brother behind, Finn. Besides, I've already got a partner." He turned to Carter. "Carter Hamilton."

Finn looked defeated but fell in line with Logan without complaint.

Carter stepped up and offered his hand. "Thanks, Bay."

The boy took his hand and gave it a firm shake. "No problem. I've noticed you keep to yourself."

Carter nodded. "Yeah, I guess it's not easy making friends."

Bay gave a sly smile. "I don't think that's your problem. I think you're a guy who sees what he wants and goes after it. Even if you are a bit obvious, I think that's a very admirable trait. One that can be respected."

Carter had never heard a kid talk that way before, and he wasn't sure if he should feel praised or insulted. "Thanks."

After that, they were inseparable, and soon after, Carter was added to the Zodiacs.

A knock came at the door, and Carter walked over and opened it to find Bay, still silver and gold from head to toe, waiting on the other side. He couldn't help but smile.

"You're in a good mood," said Bay as he stepped past Carter into the room. "I take it you had a good visit with Sin?"

"No, actually I was just thinking back to Camp V. The day we paired off as swim buddies." Carter looked at him like he might not remember, but Bay laughed.

"You know, I was already planning on recruiting you, and then you just started showing up wherever we were, like instinctively you already knew where you belonged."

Carter walked over to the bed and grabbed his suitcase. "Those were some good times, weren't they?"

Bay chuckled, walking to the window to look out at the city. "You're the only one who doesn't dwell on the bad. Everyone else sees it much differently."

Carter could understand that, but it didn't erase all of the years of happiness for him. "I guess it didn't end well, but we had some great times in those early days. They were some of the best times of my life."

"That's because you got to be away from your old man, Carter." Bay knew him like a book.

Carter couldn't disagree. "Oh, for sure. That was always part of it. But we had some crazy times. I could cut loose and not worry about being judged or condemned."

Bay walked over and gave Carter a pat on the back. "I bet it was liberating when he died."

Carter's smile faded, but not because he was insulted but because it was true. "Ken Sin hung himself in his cell. He's dead." He thought he'd go ahead and drop that bomb to change the subject.

Bay was unaffected by the news. "That's too bad, I guess. Especially for Darek. How did he take it?"

"He was pissed off. He seems to think that the case is going to heat up again."

"It could happen. But hopefully, on this trip, I'll get to do enough digging around about this Betty bitch to solve the case for him." Bay walked with him to the door and reached out for the knob, taking a moment to pause. "What do you hope to get out of it?"

"As I said, I'd like to offer my condolences to Brandy. She's been through a lot."

"That's very noble of you." Bay opened the door, and they headed out to the elevator. "I'm sure it's a huge comfort knowing she'll have all of that money to raise the baby."

"How much do you think Justin was worth?" Carter knew it was a strange turn in the conversation, but he'd always been curious. Besides, he wanted to know just how much there was to take.

"A few million at least." Bay's tone was so nonchalant, like he'd seen more money and it was nothing special. Carter wondered just how much the man had managed to earn for himself, not including his inheritance, which was upward of ten million from what he'd heard.

Carter's heart raced thinking of all the money he was going to have. He had as much right to it as Brandy did, and he would put it to far better use. As for Brandy and the baby, they'd still have a fortune to live on to send Corey's offspring to summer camp and college. She could give the baby the Farrow name and live happily ever after.

"You've got your work cut out for you," said Carter once the elevator came to a stop and they walked out into the hotel lobby.

"Yeah, the will should be mostly paperwork at this point, but the real challenge will be getting Brandy to agree to let me look around. I need access to the house and all of his important papers, cell phones, his computer."

"Do you think she'll just let you look around?"

"Yeah, I think I can be pretty persuasive." Bay looked up at him with a grin that put him on edge.

"You're not going to hurt her, are you?" He narrowed his eyes and searched Bay's reaction. He couldn't have anything happen to Brandy. She was his only link to Corey's fortune, and Bay knew nothing about that deal. It was going to stay that way too.

Bay laughed. "You really think I'd hurt her? You of all people should know I have many other ways of getting what I want." They walked out to the car, and Bay unlocked the doors.

Carter got in the passenger's seat. "You told me you'd explain this Betty person to me. Who is she?"

"We're not even sure she's a she," said Bay, sliding in behind the wheel. "She could be a *he* for all Justin knew. Betty was his online lover."

"Online?" Carter chuckled. "How do you call them a lover? How does that even work?"

"Apparently, not too well for Justin, but I would assume you'd get off from lip service. Don't tell me you never had phone sex." He started the car and then backed out as Carter processed his words.

Once Bay was on the freeway, Carter eased back in his seat for the long trip. "If he talked on the phone with her, then he should have known if it were a he or a she, right?"

"He never did. Trust me; the man had no idea who he was jerking his dick to. We have to find what evidence we can and look deeper. I know she sent him some photos, and what I want to do is see if the body parts match up and if it appears to be one true source or five or six. If there are any distinct features: moles, freckles, lumps, bumps. Anything that's going to be an identifying mark. If I can narrow it down to one source, then I can focus on the background and what kind of story it tells."

"Don't you think that Justin would have done that? He wasn't a dummy; he was just a little odd." Carter had always liked Justin's stories of cryptids and conspiracies. They were far more exciting to him than bible verses and the stories his father tried to force on him.

"Justin had no reason to be suspicious, and by the time he was, it was too late. He didn't want to see it too closely, you know? It was just a reminder of how terrible things ended, and how his dreams were crushed along with his heart."

"That sounds ridiculous when you consider he never met the person." Carter chuckled, but he also knew it was sad. Justin had been a good guy who deserved much better.

"Yeah."

Carter shifted in his seat, looking at the long road ahead. "Damn, this is going to be a long trip."

"We could have flown if you still had your jet." Bay looked as if he'd rather be on the plane than behind the wheel.

"No, this is good. It will be fun." He didn't want to talk about the church or his troubles. Admitting things were rocky wouldn't do anything but give Bay ammunition, and the ride was going to be long enough.

Bay chuckled. "Yeah, keep telling yourself that."

CHAPTER 17

DAREK

After the long morning of dealing with Sin's death, Darek thought he'd be able to return to the office and tell Lizzy all about it, but she was nowhere to be found.

The office was busy, with most of the officers hanging around chatting as if there wasn't a crime in the city that couldn't wait. Max lingered around the office too, making excess trips to the coffee bar and back to his desk. The silence between them was uncomfortable, but Darek knew better than to strike up a conversation, knowing the tension would get to Max before it did him.

"What's your problem?" he asked after the room cleared out, all but for Darius.

Darek looked over his shoulder, seeing that Max was talking to him. Darius lifted his head from the file cabinet.

"I don't think this is the time or place to discuss it," said Darek. Darius was all ears, and Darek wasn't going to let everyone in on his and Lizzy's business.

Max gave Darius a hard look until he shut the file cabinet and walked out of the room.

Darek spun around in his chair as the man left. "What's *your* problem? You really think I'm going to discuss Lizzy with you. Especially here?"

"I mean you and me. I already told you what happened, and you're still blaming me. If you want to let it get in the way of our friendship, then fine, but I thought you were better than that. Letting some chick come between us is stupid. Besides, maybe she's not the sweet and innocent you think she is?"

"Watch it, Max. I don't want to have to knock you on your ass right now."

"Please. I'd like to see you try it." He laughed. "It's true, you know? She's the one who came on to me. You wouldn't have turned down a move like that. You've taken home girls at clubs that showed you that kind of interest, even if you knew I was into them."

"That happened maybe once, and that time, you didn't tell me she was the chick you'd been pining over. If I'd known, I wouldn't have done it, okay? And I've said I'm sorry a hundred times." He couldn't believe the man was still holding a grudge after all that time. "Is that why you did it? Because of some bar skank that we are both better off without?"

"No, it wasn't about you at all. Believe it or not, I can do shit all on my own. You were a shitty partner, and you're a shitty friend."

"A shitty partner? How so? The chief would have shit-canned your ass in the first month if I hadn't been around to keep you out of trouble. You made more mistakes on the first day than most officers do in their first month."

"Fuck you. You're not Mr. Perfect. I had to keep them from sidelining your ass when you started passing out at work. I covered for you at least six times."

Darek didn't want him to bring that shit up now. "That's in the past. I'm better now."

"Yeah, and so am I because I don't have to be your partner anymore."

"Yeah, well you don't have to be my friend, either. How about that? It's not like I know you anyway. Who the fuck are you?"

"Someone who put up with your shit long enough, asshole." Max turned and walked toward the door, but he stopped short and looked back at Darek. "I know you better than anyone around this place, and you know what? I feel sorry for you. Because when this case is over, you'll see. Lizzy will be done with you too, and then you'll have no one."

Footsteps brought their heads around. Lizzy stood in the doorway, watching them. "What the hell is going on?"

"Nothing," said Max. He breezed past her and headed out.

Lizzy looked confused. "This is why I don't like taking the morning off."

"It's been a long time coming. It just happened that he found the right opportunity to tell me off." Darek shook his head and unclenched his fists. "I was two seconds away from ending that asshole."

"He was your best friend."

"We were put together. Our jobs depended on our coexistence. That's not a friendship."

She held up her hands as she approached. "Don't argue with me. Let's change the subject."

Darek sighed as she walked over, and then he looked up as she leaned in for a kiss. "I wondered where you were."

"Yeah, I thought with you doing your thing, I'd take the morning off. After you ran out on my breakfast, I sat in the kitchen quietly eating my bacon and thought that if Reed wanted me to rest, there was no better time." She smiled and brushed his hair back. "So, how was it?"

"Terrible."

"Did he slam your face into a table?" She took her chair and spun around to face him.

Darek was glad the asshole was dead for that one reason, but he knew that despite that, Lizzy wasn't going to be happy. "He's dead. Hung himself with his own pants."

She sat back in her chair. "Wow, I didn't expect that."

"Me neither. The guards said he was fine after their first check this morning, but when they went to take him down to the meeting, they found him."

"And so the song has ended," said Lizzy.

Darek nodded. "And the dance."

"So, now what? We wait until this asshole strikes again? At least with Ken Sin, we had someone to be responsible. The DA is going to have us busting ass trying to find someone to pin these murders on."

"I guess we just have to keep going over the evidence. There has to be something there. A name, something." He hoped that when Bay got back from his trip to Michigan, he'd have a lot more information on Betty and just who the person was. With any luck, he'd find something that would match up to the past victims and close the door on the case once and for all. When that happened, Darek's goal would be to silence the person before they had a chance to say anything to anyone about Virginia and Darek and the Zodiacs' past sins.

"Is that your phone?" Lizzy put her hand on his, and in the silence that followed, he heard a faint buzz as he reached in his pocket.

"Yeah." He saw the call came from the prison. "Hello?"

"Detective Blake?"

"This is Detective Blake. Who is this?"

"I'm Officer Crane from the prison. I spoke with you earlier."

"Yes. What can I do for you?"

"I think you should come down here. We found something I think you should take a look at."

"I'll be on my way." Darek hung up the phone, and Lizzy met his eyes with a curious expression. "I've got to go back down to the prison. It's something about Sin."

Lizzy stood. "I'll come along. It's not like the asshole can hurt me again."

"Okay, fine, but if Reed gets pissed, you'll get to explain."

They hurried out, and while on the way, Lizzy took his hand. "I'm sorry you didn't get your big interview this morning. I know Carter Hamilton was probably pissed he came all of this way for nothing."

"He was less than impressed. That's for sure."

They fell into silence for the rest of the trip, and when they got to the prison, Officer Crane met them at the door. "Thanks for coming so quickly. I know you'll be interested in this."

As he led them in, Darek wished he wouldn't be so vague. "What is it?"

The man smiled at Lizzy. "Hello, Agent McNamara. Are you two on this together? I thought they took you off the case after what happened. I'm glad I wasn't around to see it, or Sin would have been dead weeks ago."

Lizzy gave him a sideward glance. "We've been working on this case for some time now. What have you got for us?"

"The pants. The ones he hung himself with. They weren't his pants. His pants have gone missing."

"How can you tell? Do you have a system in place for determining that?" Darek wasn't sure how it worked.

"It's a prison, Detective. Everything had a system." He walked them into a room where the pants lay on a table.

"Have you had anyone else handle the evidence, Crane?" Darek asked.

"No, it's been handled with gloves, and we've taken the time to make sure it was well-preserved."

"Bagged and tagged, officer." Lizzy walked over to the table, and Darek had a feeling that she was going crazy over it not being logged properly. She was a stickler for details and wanted everything done by the book when it came to evidence. "Do you have any gloves?"

"No, sorry. I can get some."

Lizzy sighed. "Forget it. I don't think I'll need to touch it. But makes sure if anyone else does, that they do." She leaned in and looked at the makeshift rope. "This took time."

Darek nodded. "Our first guess was that he did this at night while the others were sleeping. Had it hidden under the covers with him, no one knowing he didn't have pants on."

"But, we know these aren't his pants. And he had to take plenty of time to make this, so what was he wearing while this was being made, and where are the other pants?"

"You wouldn't be found without your pants if you had a separate pair," said Darek. "This was staged."

"Is there any way to tell who has these issues?" asked Lizzy. "I'm guessing that one of his cellmates, maybe even the ones who beat his face, were involved."

The guard shook his head. "He'd been moved since then. The men he's with now are not our most violent offenders. We're talking petty crime and dope heads."

"Then someone was paid to do it. But who would pay anyone to off Ken Sin? I want you to look into this for me, Crane. Ask the other inmates and see if they saw or heard anything. Ripping the fabric must have taken a lot of time."

"Why not use the sheets?" asked Crane.

"They are harder to tear without a knife," said Lizzy. "They make them that way, so they're durable."

"I'll put out some feelers," said Crane. "If this was an inside job, I'll find out. The thing about prison politics is nothing is private. Someone else always knows."

Lizzy looked up at the man. "Where have you taken the body?"

"Down in our morgue for processing." Crane made a face like he hoped it wasn't too late for them to get more evidence from the body.

"Tell them to stop any procedures. I want as much of him preserved as possible and taken to Dr. Cobb. I want to make sure there aren't other interesting things about this death. I'd also like photographs of all of his tattoos."

"Do you think that our killer got to him in here?" asked Darek. It seemed highly impossible.

"I've learned not to underestimate the asshole. Whoever they are, they did this to send a message."

CHAPTER 18

BAY

After the long drive, Bay had driven them to a hotel and gotten them a two-room suite. After some complaining from Carter about the accommodations of the small town, Bay had finally gotten him to shut up by offering to pay for the room.

Then, when he had to go out and see Brandy, he insisted on coming along. As they pulled up at the bar where they'd agreed to meet up with the woman, he regretted bringing him along.

"The Sissy Bar? Does she think she's funny having us meet her at a gay bar? Is this some kind of joke?"

"No. My guess, it's a play on words. Besides, she doesn't know you're coming along. I thought you'd be a nice surprise. Now, look." Bay shot him a warning glare. "Be on your best behavior. This is a small town, and people like this are easily offended. Besides, they might recognize you."

"I'm more well-known in the south, actually, so I'll take my chances."

Bay got out of the car and went inside. Heads turned, and he didn't miss their stares, especially when Carter hurried to catch up behind him. Bay stopped and looked around, spotting the second prettiest blond in the place across the room. He walked over and greeted her with a smile.

"Brandy. It's nice to see you again."

She smiled at him until she realized who he'd brought along for the ride. "What's he doing here?" she asked with a harsh tone.

"He was in New York and wanted to come along for the ride. I hope you don't mind." He smiled inside, knowing that he'd play it off like he had no idea, and it was fun putting Carter on the spot.

"I guess it's okay. I just wasn't expecting anyone else but you." Bay could tell she was pissed off, her temper setting her nostrils into overdrive.

Bay took a seat at the table. "Charming place." The place was a dive, but he was trying his hardest with her. His job would be a hell of a lot easier if she trusted him.

She sipped her drink, which appeared to be a soda, as the men called the waitress over and ordered a couple of beers. "It was Justin's favorite."

Bay looked into her eyes as she spoke about her friend, and while there was no spark of love in them, there was adoration for the man.

"Was he a biker?" asked Carter, looking down his nose at the people around him.

Brandy sat up in her seat. "He rode. He and his friends here would host a little Sturgis rally every year to raise money. The town hated it. They don't want to be associated with bikers, but they'd take the money and ride over to the big rally in South Dakota every August and donate everything to a children's charity. He was a *good man*. Unlike some."

Bay smiled. Brandy made no bones about not liking Carter. Her tone to him alone spoke volumes, and Bay's suspicions about the two had to be spot on.

"Yes, and a good friend," said Bay. "He and Corey both deserved much better than the hands they were dealt. I know that Corey would be so proud of his child."

Brandy put a protective hand on her belly. "I can meet you tomorrow to sign all the papers if that works for you."

"I'll call with the time. I want us to go over every inch so that you understand everything."

"It should be easy, right? I sign the papers, and everything, the house, the businesses, the cars, they're all mine?"

"For the most part." He shrugged like it was no big deal. "I'll need access to Justin's personal files and his computer."

She laughed. "You think I don't know what you're really looking for, Bay?"

Bay took his beer from the waitress's tray and took a sip. "Why don't you enlighten me, sweetheart?"

She produced a picture from her purse and put it down on the table. The rosy nipples in the photo were a soft pink but demanded attention. It was easy to see why Justin might fall in love with the mystery girl. "There are more like it," she continued. "All close shots, all vague, nothing special."

"What do you know about it?" asked Bay.

"Enough," she said.

Bay glanced at Carter, whose eyes widened. "If they are so vague and useless, then you'll have no trouble letting me have them. You wouldn't want anything getting out about Corey or Justin, tarnishing their good names, your child's name."

She seemed content with herself. "I'll think about it. Come out to the house tomorrow, and once the papers are signed, I might let you look around. I'd like to make this as quick as possible. I'll be putting the businesses up for sale."

"What about the house?" asked Bay. "Do you intend to live there?"

"I'm going to keep it, but no. I can't live there with too many memories; things I can't get out of my mind."

Bay knew that Justin had a panic room from the information disclosed in the will. The man had even gone as far as to draw a map. He had really trusted Lane Simon with his business, but thankfully, it had fallen in Bay's lap. "I don't blame you, Brandy. Please know that if there is anything I can do for you or the baby, all you have to do is reach out. Corey and Justin were my brothers."

"Is that what you call each other?" She smiled, and Bay was about to take it the wrong way, when she added, "Corey once told me he thought the same of you." She gave him a sweet smile.

"We've been through a lot together."

"I can imagine. I saw their scars. The ones they had on their shoulders. I always thought they looked so painful. It must have meant a lot to them. Corey said you all had one."

Bay took her hand and put it to his collar. Then he slipped it inside and let her feel the flesh that was close to his gunshot wound. Her cool fingers traced the outline of his mark.

"Scorpio," he said with a smile.

"Corey was Gemini. I used to think that Justin was obsessed with sixty-nine, from his Cancer brand." She giggled then turned to Carter. "What are you?"

"Leo, the lion." He met her eyes and could tell that he was trying hard to look intimidating.

"The cowardly lion," said Bay with a wink.

Carter sneered. "You know better." He appeared less and less fazed by the two of them.

Brandy leaned forward, and Bay couldn't help but notice her rack. Brandy noticed him looking too. "How's Mia?"

"She's on her way to her sister's. She's had a rough time lately, but she's doing well."

"Aw. You should have brought her along. But that sounds like fun. I'm afraid I've been so busy with the stores to get away yet. But soon, I need it. I know Corey would want me to keep on going. We talked about traveling and raising our kids on the road. But now, I'll be lucky to catch a break until I sell."

"It's good you can step in and help out at the stores."

"Yeah, but not for long. I'm selling as soon as possible. They are way too much work for a single mother."

Bay wasn't going to tell her about the fact that she didn't own the stores. He would save that surprise for later.

A song came on the jukebox, and she covered her mouth. "Corey and I loved this song."

Bay looked over to where a few other couples were moving to the music. "Would you like to dance? We could pay our friend some respect."

"That would be nice." Her face lit up, and she took his hand.

As they made their way out onto the floor, Carter stayed behind, sipping his drink.

By the time the song was over, Brandy was in tears, and Bay took the opportunity to hold her and endear her to him. So, when the slow song came on right after, he pulled her close and let her cry on his shoulder.

"It's okay. Let it all out." He really didn't care so much if she was broken up inside, and that would only make dealing with her that much easier, but he also wanted her to think he was a good man, one she could possibly play. It would make getting his way that much more fun.

After they danced to another two songs, Brandy looked up at him and then kissed his cheek. "Thank you," she said. "You're such a good guy, Bay. You come across so strong that I didn't expect you to sweep me out to the dance floor and let me cry on your shoulder."

"I get it all the time," he said with a wink. "Besides, we've been through a lot together. Not many people can say they met in a drive-by."

She gave a half-hearted smile. "True."

He walked her back to their table where Carter was chatting it up with one of the waitresses.

"I really need to get back home," she said. "I only stay out here so late to avoid being alone in that house."

Bay was all over it. He wondered how easy it would be to get the woman to spread her legs for him. He liked fucking pregnant women, and besides, he'd do anything to break her down even more. "You get some rest, and call me if you need me. I'm staying across town in the hotel." There was only one hotel, and she should know which one. "I could be there in a flash if you need me." He brushed her hair back and kissed her forehead.

"Walk me to my car?" she asked. "Or are you boys going to stay out and get into some trouble?"

"We might have another drink." He noticed the way that Carter was eyeing the trashy local.

He walked Brandy out to her car, and after another hug, she got in the car and drove away.

Before Bay could walk back inside, Carter came out of the bar, shaking his head. "I tell you, you're a smooth motherfucker. Trying to get in her pants on the first night in town. Although you didn't succeed, so you must be losing your touch."

"Nope, I have her right where I want her. If we're lucky, this will be the last night in that shitty hotel, and we'll be staying at Casa de Finch."

"You really think she's going to let us stay with her?"

"Maybe not you. She doesn't like you. Isn't that strange? It was almost like she wanted to punch you in the face. Why could that be? You barely know her, right?"

Carter shifted uncomfortably on his feet. "I only barely knew her from the hospital. Maybe she doesn't want my prayers." They walked to the car, and as he walked around to the other side, Bay called over the roof of the car before he got in.

"You know, for someone who came to offer prayers, you never mentioned it. Are you sure you didn't come for a different reason?" He thought he'd give the man one last chance to own up to what he was up to.

"What other reason would I come for? I hardly felt like the sleazy bar was the right place to start a prayer circle. I mean, don't get me wrong. It would have been awesome, but I'm not out to embarrass her. I don't even know her religion."

"Comfort knows no religious bounds, my friend." He had been about as comforting as burlap to a sunburn.

CHAPTER 19

DAREK

Darek's day hadn't gotten any better after talking to Sin's cellmates. None of them knew a damned thing. The case was taking a strange turn. He'd gone from searching for the Zodiac killer to finding out who killed Ophi.

To make matters worse, when he left work and tried to relax his brain, he had no luck. It wasn't the case that was bothering him so much but the way things had gone down with him and Max.

Even though the man was a pain in the ass, he had been one of Darek's best friends, and they'd shared some special moments. He couldn't let the night end without making shit right, and there was only one way he knew how to do that with Max.

He dialed his number and waited for him to answer.

"Hey, asshole." The insult was only half-hearted from the sound of his voice, and Darek let it slide.

"I was wondering if you wanted to go out and have a beer? I'm in the area. I'll pick you up."

Max sounded hurried. "I'm not home, man. I'm just leaving the gym."

"I could come and get you. It's no problem. Unless you don't want to go?" He had to face the fact that Max might not want to make up with him. Things had gotten pretty ugly between them. And some things were said that neither could take back.

"How about I meet you at Ginny's Pub?" asked Max.

"That sound's good. I'll see you there. I'll buy the first round."

The call ended, and Darek took the next street and made his way a few blocks over to Ginny's where there was never any parking. By the time he drove around and finally found a spot, Max met him out front.

Darek walked up and offered his hand, and Max reluctantly took it, giving it a firm squeeze. "Look, man, I said some shit I wished I wouldn't have."

"Me too," said Max. "Let's stop talking about it like two bitches and go and get fucked up."

"Agreed." That was exactly what Darek needed after the shitty day he'd had, and the two went inside and found two seats at the bar.

Max sat down next to a gorgeous blonde who licked her lips and turned her stool in his direction. "I'm Hilly," she said. "Want to go back to my place for some fun?" She directed the question at the two of them, and Darek shook his head and grinned.

"No, thanks, baby," said Max. "We've already had one woman come between us. Besides, this one prefers brunettes."

"I could be a brunette," she said with a bubbly voice. She'd had too much to drink already and leaned over on Max's arm. "What do you prefer?"

Max looked her square in the eyes. "Sanity."

As the two men shared a chuckle, the bartender came over, and they called out their usual poison. Two seconds later, they had their drinks, and Max turned his up.

Darek didn't think much of it, but when the man hit three beers before Darek could finish his first, he had to wonder if Max really was going to get fucked up. The two had pulled some shit in their past, but Darek couldn't fuck anything up with his promotion so close he could taste it.

With all of their tension, he decided to let it go and just let Max have his fun.

"I'll win the table if you want to play," Max said, looking across the room at the pool table.

Darek clapped him on the back. "Sounds fun. It's been a long time since I beat your ass at pool."

Max laughed. "That's because it rarely happened. Maybe once or twice when you were lucky and I was distracted by pussy."

"That was almost every night if I remember correctly." Darek had been married most of their time as pals, but Max had enough women for the two of them.

"Watch this." He walked up and put his quarters on the table.

The men who were playing couldn't believe it. "Really, Max? You're going to take our table?"

"Hey, I'll let you play with me." He shook their hands as Darek tried to recall their names. It wasn't important that he didn't remember because as soon as their game was over, they left.

"It's all yours," said the one who Darek thought might be named Paul.

Max walked over and patted the man on the back. "Come on, Paul, are you too scared to shoot a game with me?"

"Your drunk ass is going to take us all to jail again, and this time, you'll be in the cell with me. That last time was too much, you bastard."

The group of men laughed, and Paul put his arm around his girl, and they made their way out of the bar.

Max turned and looked Darek dead in the eyes. His glassy stare was ringed red. "Those guys love me." He had spent more time at the bar than Darek for sure, and while Darek had been hanging solo at the river, drinking alone, Max had made new friends.

Maybe they didn't know each other so well anymore. Both of their lives had taken different directions, and the only thing they'd had in common for years was their job and the fact that they were stuck in a car with each other every day.

After that, Darek and Max played pool and darts, and by the end of their third round, Max could barely stand without wobbling. The only thing he managed was not spilling his beer, which greatly impressed Darek.

He aimed the last dart. "Watch this," he said to the blonde who had followed him over to the dartboard. She hung on his shoulder as he tried to line up his throw and accidentally made a shot bounce off of the board. The dart went flying and hit a man on the back. That was when the fight was on.

"Watch what you're doing, drunk-ass motherfucker." The man was about two inches taller than Max and had about six more in reach.

Max took a few good swings but only connected with one, compared to the two that he took. Darek stepped in to stop it and finally had to pull his badge. "That's enough."

The woman, who had been hanging all over Max half the night, bailed as soon as she saw the badge.

"Fucking cops," said the man. "You're pathetic." He spat at Max's feet, and then as he walked away, Max jumped on his back.

It took Darek five minutes to get the man to stop turning him around, and when he did, Max fell to the floor and puked.

"Get your pussy friend out of here," said the man. "Before I mop his puke with his face."

Darek grabbed Max and pulled him up to his feet as the man kept mouthing off. "Fucking pussies, that's all they are." The crowd around them wasn't in agreement, and when Darek knocked the fuck out of the loudmouth with a single punch, the entire bar cheered, including Max who was barely clinging to consciousness.

"Fuck," said Darek. "Let's get you home, man." He shook his hand and hoped that he hadn't broken anything. He wasn't sure how he would explain what had happened to Lizzy if that were the case.

Darek picked him up and walked him out to the car where he put him in the backseat. He hoped Max didn't puke again and got in the front and started the car. He hurried down the road a few blocks where Max lived, and when he pulled up at his house, he killed the engine and tried to wake him.

He had done this dance with Max more times than he could remember, so he fished his keys from his pocket and picked him up, carrying him close. Max was a good drunk walker, and that made it easier for Darek to get him in the house and to his bedroom.

He stopped at the foot of his bed and noticed the stack of clothes. Max had the habit of laying out his clothes and shoes for work, and Darek pushed them aside and put him down as gently as possible on top of the covers.

He took a few deep breaths to steady himself and then walked to the kitchen.

After carrying him all that way, his mouth had gone dry, so he went to get a drink of water. As he opened the fridge, he looked at the calendar hanging on the door. The thing had notes all over it, but one stuck out to Darek.

NOLA flight 11 a.m.

It had been circled in red ink and heavily underlined, and it was written in the day of the shooting in New Orleans. Warning bells sounded in Darek's ears.

Max had said he was out of town around then, but he'd claimed he'd gone to Tennessee where he was supposed to visit some family. Darek remembered that he hadn't gotten along with them too well and remembered feeling odd about the way Max acted when questioned about it.

His phone ringing in his pocket turned his attention away as Lizzy called.

He answered it on his way out, still stunned by what he found and not sure he should mention it to anyone. "Hey, baby."

"Hey, you. Where were you? I came by after kickboxing, and you weren't around."

"I needed a little time with Max." Even though the man had passed out drunk, Darek felt better that they wouldn't be at each other's throats anymore.

"Don't tell me the two of you were fighting again." There was disappointment in her tone, and Darek couldn't help still feeling a little bitter about all that had happened.

"No, we had a few beers and worked it out."

"So that's where you've been. Are you home now?"

Darek went out to his car and got in. "No, I'm leaving Max's house. He was sloppy drunk, and I had to put him to bed."

"Are you sloppy drunk too?"

Darek thought about how bad off Max had been, blowing chunks all over the bar. "Not as bad, no. I'll be fine. I was going to tell you that Cobb never texted to tell me that Sin's body had arrived."

"I could call and check on it. You're not too bad off to drive, are you? Do you need me to come and pick you up?"

"No, I'm good. Seriously, baby, don't worry about me. I've always held my liquor much better than most of my friends." He knew the trick was not overdoing it. He only pulled that kind of shit when he was heartbroken.

"Fine, I guess I have no reason to come over."

"I didn't say that. I'm a perfect reason to come over, don't you think?" He tried not to laugh as he wanted to sound insulted.

Lizzy cracked. She giggled, and her voice was so sweet that he got aroused.

"I could stop by," he suggested.

She made a sound of frustration. "The place is a wreck, but I don't mind if you want to pick me up."

She rarely wanted to stay at her place, but Darek wouldn't argue. He liked his place better anyway. He hated waking up to Bob's criticizing looks or worse, the cat's ass in his face. "I'll be there in about five minutes."

With one last giggle into the phone, she whispered, "I'll be waiting."

He hung up the phone and smiled, pleased that the day had ended much better than it began. He just couldn't stop thinking about that note on Max's calendar and decided to ask Lizzy about it when he got to her place. Why would Max have any reason to lie about where he'd been?

He knew where I was going. No, you're thinking crazy shit, man. "Get it together, Detective."

CHAPTER 20

CARTER

The long road to Justin's property reminded Carter of something he'd seen in a horror film once when he was about eleven. That had also been the last time he'd watched a horror film, and he swore he'd never get caught out in the middle of nowhere with a psycho.

He looked over at Bay, who was eased back in the driver's seat with the window down and the wind in his hair.

Too late.

"We need to turn around and call Brandy," said Carter. "I'm not sure that we aren't lost."

"We're not. Brandy told me to keep going and that we might feel like we're never going to find it."

He couldn't help but wonder if she had something up her sleeve. Was she leading them down the long road to the middle of nowhere so she could kill them and they'd never be found? He wondered if he should call his elder and tell him where he was, but he knew that Bay would skin him alive and wear his head as a hat if he did.

He just didn't trust Brandy, and he didn't like being stuck depending on her for anything, not even directions. The only saving grace was that the reason they were going out was to make her a very rich woman, and while she already was, she wasn't going to balk at the millions Justin had left her.

Just as he was about to complain again, Bay pointed up ahead. "See, she wasn't fucking with us."

"That's Justin's house?" Carter could not believe the beautiful home that was waiting in the woods. The cabin had a wraparound porch and a huge workshop off to one side that matched the main house, and it was beautifully landscaped. The view in the backyard was breathtaking, with a winding creek in the distance and beautiful flowering bushes. "It's gorgeous."

Bay gave a nod. "Yeah, it's such a shame. He spent so much time and money building the place, only to be shot down in the middle of it." Bay pulled the car to a stop and killed the engine.

Brandy walked out onto the porch as they got out of the car, and the sounds of birds chirping were like heaven until she opened her mouth. "Did you get lost?" She wasn't talking to him, but Bay. And she had a big smile for him as well.

"No, you were a genius with those directions." Bay stepped up to the house with his briefcase in hand, and Carter picked up the rear. He watched as the two checked each other out, and Brandy stepped aside and let Bay walk to the door ahead of her.

She gave Carter a hard look as he approached and stepped in front of him. Carter couldn't blame her for being less than hospitable to him. He was, after all, there to take half of her windfall, and he had no intention on even waiting for the ink to be dry on her paperwork before letting her know his intentions.

"I take it you've brought all of the papers?"

"Every last one. Your pretty hands might get tired, but I'll work out the soreness for you." He gave her a wink as Carter wanted to vomit.

"You men have a seat, and I'll get you some lemonade." She disappeared into the kitchen.

Bay took a seat on the couch and put his briefcase on the coffee table. "I'll get our papers ready, and we'll get started," he said calling to her.

She returned and placed the tray on the table beside the sofa. "You men just help yourself."

"Thank you," said Bay, passing her a stack of papers. "This is the will. Then I have papers regarding the house."

"What about the stores?"

"I'm still waiting on a few things to be signed at the bank, but I should have those soon. Did you have something more for me, Brandy?"

She reached into her handbag and pulled out Justin's phone. Then she passed it to Bay and took out a laptop. "I took a quick look through the laptop," she said. "There's nothing there. And here are the photographs. There are more on the computer and the phone. Whoever she is, she had no problem sending plenty of nudes."

Bay took the stack of photos and flipped through them. "Do you mind if I take these and the laptop to the hotel and look them over, or would you prefer I stay here with them? It could take hours. Possibly into the night."

Carter remembered what Bay had said about them staying the night and having the run of the house.

"You could stay as long as you want and check over the laptop, but I'd prefer you not take it. A lot of the store files are there, and I need them for payroll this next week."

"I understand. It's not a problem. I'll send some of the things I need to my email."

Carter got to his feet and walked over to stare out the window. When he turned around, he caught the woman glaring at him.

Brandy turned her attention to Bay. "I know it seems like I'm being silly. I do apologize. I'm just not used to company, and Justin was a private person."

"It's understandable." Bay reached out to touch her arm.

Brandy and Bay both gave him a hard glare.

"I'll just be outside." He walked out the door and closed it behind him, and as he paced back and forth on the porch, he would glance through the window to see what they were up to.

After a while of roaming the yard, he realized that she might tell Bay what he was up to and hurried back inside.

Bay sat on the couch with all of the photos scattered across the table in front of him while he looked through the phone. The computer was open next to him, and there were tits and snatch on display.

Brandy sat in her chair reading the will and didn't bother to look up as he walked back into the room.

Bay waved him over. "Look at these. Do any of them look like they don't belong?"

"Which is not like the other," Carter whispered as he leaned over the back of the couch and looked at the body parts.

"They are pretty consistent, aren't they?" Bay picked up two different tit shots and held them side by side.

"I think you're right," said Carter. "This is the same girl. She's blonde."

"Carpet matches the drapes," said Bay. "Let's look for every photo that shows some background. I'm pretty sure that we can put them together like a puzzle and get something."

"This looks like everything is in order," Brandy said. "I just want to see the store stuff before I sign anything."

Bay stretched his arms. "I hate to get too comfortable on the computer and start on the other photos until I get a few things I left at the hotel that I need for overnight."

"I'll finish reading over the house papers while you're gone," said Brandy, getting to her feet.

Bay and Carter got up, and while Bay fished out his keys, Carter realized he didn't want to go. He needed a minute there to talk to Brandy without Bay.

As they walked out, he followed Bay to the driver's side. "Hey, do you mind grabbing my phone charger?"

"You're not going with me? I think we need to talk." Bay unlocked the door and gestured for him to get in the car.

Carter hesitated but finally agreed, and when they were alone in the car with the engine started, Bay let out a deep breath. "She knows too fucking much about us, Carter. All of those messages in the phone, the photographs, she even admitted it."

"I thought you were a little too nice. What are you getting at, Bay?"

Bay took a deep breath and looked him in the eye. "You know what has to be done."

Carter was outraged. "Wait, you want to kill her?"

Bay looked at him like he was the insane one. "What else do you suggest? She knows about us, Carter."

Carter didn't know how to react to what Bay was suggesting, but he couldn't let him take Brandy out. All of the money had to come through her. She was the only one who had access to Corey's money, but Bay had no idea about that. If Carter was going to protect her from Bay, he would have to explain why. And that would mean splitting the money.

"I can't be a part of that, Bay. I mean, look at her. She's pregnant."

"How do we know she is? She isn't showing or anything. She might be lying to play on our sympathies, and that's a chance I'm willing to take. Unless you can tell me another reason that we should keep her alive, I'm waiting until she's asleep and I'm going to slit her throat."

"But what about all of Justin's money? What happens to it then?"

"Money? You're concerned about the money when this person, this gold-digging trash, could ruin us?"

"If she wanted to do that, she would have already, right?"

Bay shrugged. "Not until she's done with us. She sure seems to hate you. Why is that?" He gave him an accusing look.

Carter was scrambling. "Maybe she's against preachers. I don't know. Maybe she's been abused by one in the past, or I look too much like someone who abused her."

Bay turned and looked ahead. Then he backed out of the drive and turned onto the road. "I'm disappointed in you, Carter."

His back stiffened at Bay's tone. Those were the four words he never wanted to hear from Bay. Even as a kid, it could only mean bad things. "Bay, it's wrong. And I thought you said you weren't going to kill her."

Bay sped down the long drive, taking them nearly a mile from the house before he pulled over. "That's before I realized what a threat she was. But you? You're not telling me the truth. I can feel it, Carter. You're keeping secrets."

"No. I'm not Bay. I wouldn't fuck you over. I wouldn't do anything to hurt the group, especially when there are so few of us left."

"Get out."

"What?"

"We're done with our talk, and you wanted to stay, so get out. You can walk back to the house." He shrugged like it was nothing and kept his eyes forward.

Carter opened the car door, knowing better than to try and change his mind.

"One more thing," said Bay before Carter shut the door. "While you're on the way back, I'd strongly consider what it means to lie to me. Because if I find out that you're holding out on me, I'm not going to be a happy man, Carter."

Carter looked down at his shoes, which were hardly made for more than showing off on stage, and he let out a growl of frustration. "Fine!" He got back into the car and slammed the door, fully prepared to spill his guts, but part of the truth just couldn't be spoken. "I came because Justin owes me money. I want to make Brandy pay up. I don't see why I have to suffer because he's dead."

"Why didn't you just tell me that? I could make sure that you get your money. How much was it?" Bay's tone was bad, but Carter felt a bit of relief that he might actually buy it.

Carter wasn't about to leave with a measly twenty-thousand. "Does it matter?"

"It does if you want to collect it. I know how much she had and what she hasn't."

"Two million."

Bay laughed. "Justin owed you two million dollars? I somehow doubt that, but okay. Get out."

"Wait, why? I told you the truth." He had hoped the man would at least take pity and drive him back to the house.

"Two million is a lot of money. I'd take this time to make sure you secure it."

"You don't understand, Bay. I need her alive long enough to collect, and then I don't give a fuck what happens to her."

Bay put his arm across the back of the seat and leaned in closer. "I tell you what. I'll help you out of this mess, and I won't kill her, but you're going to have to make sure I'm well compensated."

"I can do that. How's twenty-thousand?" He held his breath and hoped that the amount wouldn't insult him.

Bay shrugged like it sounded okay to him. "I'll think about it. You better get moving. I need to go and check us out. I'll be sure to grab all of your shit."

Carter got out of the car but hesitated a minute. "Don't forget to grab my phone charger and toothbrush please."

"Sure thing, man." Bay smiled, and Carter breathed a sigh of relief. He thought Bay might ask for more when the time came, but he'd worry about that later. He had to make sure Brandy knew he wasn't leaving until things were in order.

He shut the car door, and Bay sped away, throwing up dust behind him. "Fucking asshole."

He walked the long road back to the house, and by the time he was there, he was thirsty and needed a drink. He walked back up on the porch and knocked on the door. "Brandy, it's me." He pounded and peeked through the window, but she wasn't anywhere in sight. "Brandy!"

Finally, she rounded the corner from the hall and rolled her eyes. She came over and opened the door. "What are you doing here? Where's Bay?"

"He's gone to the hotel, but I changed my mind." Carter breezed past her as she stepped aside and opened the door wider. "I told him I'd stay and get a jump start on those papers."

"He doesn't know about your plans, does he? How you're extorting money from me, my unborn child, and his dead friends?"

"Don't let Bay fool you, sweetie. You're a means to an end for him and nothing more. He just wants his information." He didn't want her to think that Bay would actually like her type.

"He seems a lot nicer than you."

"I want the money for my church."

"I thought the church was supposed to help widows and orphans, not the other way around."

"If the widow is sitting on a big pile of money that she didn't earn honestly and that she could never spend, why not spread that around?"

"Listen to you. You really believe that bullshit, don't you? I mean, I've heard of men believing in their own lies, but you really think you're doing some good."

Carter shrugged.

"I don't buy it," said Brandy. "Not for one fucking minute. If it's a donation you want, I'd gladly give it, but you're planning on sticking me for half of Corey's money."

"Well, that's sort of right." Carter met her eyes and saw the moment she realized what he had come for.

"You came to see how much I was getting from Justin, too. You want a bigger share, don't you?"

"Yes, and yes. And I thought about you going all the way to Phoenix. I can't see you coming back empty-handed. I know if it were me, I'd have brought back a good wad of cash. So, I'd like a down payment of good faith."

"Good faith?" She laughed. "Are you kidding me?"

"No, I'm quite serious. And don't discuss any of this with Bay."

"You don't want him to know what a crooked vulture you are? Circling around and waiting for a corpse so you can pick my bones clean."

"No. I was thinking more like you shouldn't tell him so he doesn't want his cut. It wouldn't do you any better to have to split things three ways. And since so far, I'm the only one with any dirt on you, I'm your only enemy."

Brandy let out a breath of frustration. "Fine, I'll give you ten-grand in cash, and that's it. I don't have anymore. You can get the rest in your account as you talked about before."

He walked over and sat on the couch in front of the photographs. "Sounds good to me."

CHAPTER 21

DAREK

The phone's vibrations on the table beside Darek's head were worse than any alarm clock. He popped his head up and reached over to get it before it woke Lizzy up too. But as he leaned back against his pillow, he realized that the bed was cold beside him.

Lizzy was gone.

Not knowing if she'd gone back home to Bob and her bed, he answered the phone, knowing he'd look for her after. "Hello?"

"Detective Blake, this is Officer O'Brien. We have a report of a body found. A young woman. I've got a crew on the way, but I thought I'd call and let you know. The initial report was a stabbing, but they also said there was so much blood, that they couldn't be sure that's all."

"Shit. Thanks, man. Text me the location, and I'll be right there."

"You got it."

Darek ended the call and scratched his chest as he let out a big yawn. "Lizzy?" He waited to see if she would respond, but she didn't. Instead, he heard a noise from the kitchen. A slight movement.

He got to his feet and walked into the room, turning on the light. "Lizzy?"

She poked her head around from the kitchen. "Hey, sorry if I woke you up."

"You didn't. What are you doing in here?"

"Just looking for something to eat. I woke up, and my stomach was growling. I hope you don't mind me raiding your fridge." She gave him a shy look, and he pulled her in for a kiss.

After their lips met briefly, he pulled away and brushed her hair back from her face. "I'm afraid we've been called in." He glanced down, and she had her phone in her hands. "Did you get one too?"

"No, not yet," she said as she looked down at the screen. "I was using my phone for a flashlight."

Darek walked away, heading back to his room. "Don't be surprised when they do. We've got a body. Stabbing they think."

"Shit. Sounds all too familiar." Lizzy hurried and was behind him by the time he got to the bedroom. She pulled off his T-shirt and found her jeans and the top she'd worn over.

"Yeah, I thought so too." He pulled on some pants and then walked to the closet.

"Man or woman?" asked Lizzy.

"Woman. It sounds like it just came in."

Lizzy grabbed her bag and strapped on her gun. Darek checked his Glock as they headed to the door. They stopped there to put on their shoes and then headed out to the car.

"Damn it. What time is it?" Darek hadn't expected to see the sun because his house was still dark, but there was still no sign of the sun even on the horizon.

"It's four-forty in the morning."

He got into his car and unlocked the door for Lizzy. "It's too early for this shit." He passed her his phone once they were both inside. "Here, O'Brien was supposed to text me the location. See where we're going."

She moved her fingers across the screen. "Three-thirty Elm."

"Wait, what?" Darek's face flushed. The address was too familiar.

"Three-thirty Elm. Do you know it?"

"Yeah."

Lizzy put her hand on his leg and leaned in toward him. "Shit. Who is it?"

Darek shook his head. *It can't be. She's gone out of town. She wasn't coming back this soon.*

"Darek, you're scaring me. Get out; I'm driving. You're as pale as a ghost."

"It's Raven's house."

"What? You're kidding me?" Lizzy closed her eyes. "Shit, Darek. I'm so sorry."

He closed his eyes. "Let's just get there." He got out of the car, and Lizzy slid over. She put the pedal down and backed out of his drive before speeding off toward that part of town.

Darek tried to keep it together. He held his breath and hoped that it was a mistake.

When they got there, he jumped out of the car, but Lizzy ran to hold him back. "No, Darek. You're not rushing in there too emotional. You're going to let me go inside and check it out."

"Lizzy, I gotta see if it's her." Tears welled in his eyes, and he felt horrible for showing the emotions in front of her.

"It's okay. I'm not leaving your side."

He went up the path to the house from the street, and it was the longest walk of his life. It was as if the path had stretched out, growing longer with each step.

The officer at the door opened it, and Darek didn't miss the concerned look in his eyes as the man stepped aside and let him through.

The house was the same. Nothing of Raven's had changed much, aside from the bright red that may as well have been a neon sign flashing like a warning. His heart beat so fast in his chest that it drowned out all sound as he moved closer.

The victim's dark hair was soaked in blood and covering her face. No one had even touched her yet. Darek knelt down and carefully moved the matted mess from her eyes, the blood soaking his fingertips.

"It's not her," said Lizzy.

Darek couldn't stop staring at the woman's face. It wasn't Raven, but it looked an awful lot like her. Same nose, same dark hair and beautiful lips. "Has the homeowner been notified?" He knew that Raven had leased the place, and while she had been having a tough time getting her rent paid with all of the drama in her life, she would have never broken the lease agreement.

"Not yet," said O'Brien. "We haven't been here for more than forty minutes now. The body was still pretty warm when we got here."

"I'll call her if you want me to," said Lizzy.

"I should be the one. I owe her that much." He gave Lizzy an apologetic look.

"Hey, don't worry about it, okay? This is a horrible situation, but she'll be fine. Call her. I'll just be talking with O'Brien." She walked away, and Darek took out his phone.

He walked over and leaned against the wall for support. The grueling seconds before he knew it wasn't her had wrecked him. It had also made him question everything. He pushed it all out of his mind and dialed her number, praying that she hadn't changed it.

It rang three times before she picked up, and while he breathed a sigh of relief hearing her hello, now came the harder part.

"Raven?"

"Darek. Hey. I didn't expect to hear from you so soon, especially so early in the morning." Her voice was sleepy, and he realized he'd woken her up.

"I'm calling on official business, Rave." He looked over at the body. "I'm at your house."

"Oh no, what has Honey done this time? Please don't take her in, Darek."

"Your cousin, Honey, the waitress?" Darek had heard her mention Honey, who had been as close as a sister to her.

"Yes. I'm letting her stay at the apartment and—"

"I'm sorry, Raven. She's dead." Darek knew he had to get to the point of the call, or he'd never be able to say it. There wasn't a way to do it painlessly.

"What? No!" Raven's scream of pain was enough to make the lump in Darek's throat grow bigger. "What happened?"

"She was stabbed. Someone came in here, and I think that they thought she was you."

"No. No." She wept, and Darek wished he could hold her. She had gotten too close to them all, and now she had paid for it.

"I'm sorry."

"How's Noah, is he okay?" she asked in a rush of breath.

"Noah?"

Her voice was growing more anxious. "Her son. He is staying there with her. Did he see who it was?"

"There's no one here, Raven." Darek knew better than to panic too quickly. "Is there anyone who might be babysitting the boy?"

Her voice grew even more strained with tears. "No," she squealed. "He's only four. She works at the event center, so she brings him with her, and she doesn't trust sitters. She barely let me watch him." She wept as she tried to hold her breath. "Do you think they took him?"

"Fuck. Stay on the line, okay, baby?" He handed the phone to the nearest officer. "Don't let her off the line!" He walked to the center of the room. "Listen up," he shouted. "Did anyone check this house for anyone else? We're missing a young boy. His name is Noah. He's four years old."

He met Lizzy's gaze, and while she didn't look too happy to begin with, her eyes went wide with fear.

Darek looked over to the corner of the room where there was a little toy truck that should have been a tell-tale sign. "Spread out. Look everywhere."

The house wasn't that big, and Darek hurried down the hall to check the other rooms and went to Raven's bedroom to peek under the bed. There wasn't anyone hiding there or in the closet either. He walked past the bathroom door and stepped on a stuffed monkey doll. He picked it up and called out the boy's name. He had a feeling he was close. "Noah?"

The other officers were doing the same across the house and in the kitchen and the other bathroom, but Darek had a feeling the boy had been sleeping in the same room as his mother. "Noah, it's Detective Blake. I'm here to help you." He stepped into the bathroom and saw the shower curtain drawn, the faucet still dripping into a shallow filled tub. Darek's heart dropped to his feet. He wasn't sure if the child was going to be there in that water behind that curtain.

He put his hand over his mouth and approached. And with one deep breath, he pulled back the curtain.

The tub was full of toys and action figures floating on the surface, one posed in a toy boat that was blocking the drain. Darek reached down and moved the toy, and the rest of the water started to flow. The water was freezing and must have been left that way since bath time.

The floor was covered with a makeshift rug, a single towel spread out, and laundry scattered the floor. While he stood there thinking, he heard something clicking, a soft chattering sound and then a breath. He turned his head and looked at the hamper.

Darek knew he had to move slowly. He could see a little finger sticking out of the lid and breathed a sigh of relief. "Noah?" he asked with a soft voice.

Lizzy walked into the room behind him. "Any luck?"

He held up his hand then brought a finger to his lips. "Noah, I'm a police officer. Raven told me you were here. That she needed me to find you and make sure you were safe."

Darek watched the hamper, and the little boy slowly pulled his finger inside with him.

Lizzy's eyes widened. "Noah? I'm Lizzy. Would you please come out of the hamper and talk to me?"

"I want Mama," said the boy.

"She's not able to come in here, Noah, but she wanted me to come and get you. We're going to have to call Raven. You like her, don't you? Isn't she a part of your family?"

"Auntie Raven went away too." The little fellow's teeth chattered as he trembled.

"No, I have her on the phone," said Darek. He rushed out of the room and waved to the officer who was babysitting the phone. He hurried back in to see the little boy peeking out of the top. His eyes were red and swollen from crying and full of terror. Strangely enough, he reminded Darek of Tad.

"Raven, we found Noah. He's safe, but he's really scared. I'm not sure what he knows, but I need you to talk to him."

Darek listened to Raven's sobs.

After a moment, she calmed down a bit. "Okay, put Monkey on the phone."

"He won't take it; I'll put it on speaker." Darek turned the phone to speaker mode, and Raven called out to the boy.

"Noah? It's me, Auntie Rave. I'm going to need you to go with the nice man. His name is Darek Blake, and he's a policeman. He'll make sure you're safe, baby." Her voice broke again, the tears making her sniffle.

After some more coaxing, the little boy raised up out of the hamper and held out his arms to Darek. He passed the phone to Lizzy and picked up the child, hugging him tightly. "Your Auntie Rave is a good friend of mine," he told the boy. "I'll make sure you're safe until she can get you. I promise."

Lizzy passed him the phone and hurried out of the bathroom. Darek could tell that she was emotional about more than just the shit happening around her. He took the phone off speaker and held it to his ear. "When can you be here, Raven?"

He carried the little boy to the bedroom with him to find a blanket. Noah's mother was lying in a puddle of her own blood in the middle of the house, and while Darek wasn't sure what the boy had seen, he wasn't about to let him see it again.

"Today. I'll take the next flight and be there as soon as I can. Will they let me take him?"

"Yes, I'll make sure of it." He put the kid down on the bed and wrapped a blanket around him. "We'll sit here a minute while I talk to your auntie, okay?"

The little boy nodded.

Raven made a sound of frustration. "I'll have to get a hotel room."

He could tell she was scrambling for what to do. "I'll loan you the money if you're strapped." He knew that with her losing her job after the shooting, she didn't have a lot of money.

"It's just a bad time. I'm broke. I just sent out my rent and the back rent that I owed."

"Hey, this stuff never happens when we're prepared. Do you need me to buy you a ticket? I have you covered, okay?"

"I'll pay you back." She said in a soft voice. "Thank you for being there for him."

He didn't like the idea of her going to a hotel, especially if the murder was meant for her. "I'll make sure you have a guard, too. That you're both safe."

"I'm not worried about me," she said. "I'm worried about Noah. What will happen to him?"

He took a few steps away from the boy and lowered his voice. "I won't let him out of my sight unless I know where he is and who he's with. They are going to want to question him, Raven. Hopefully, he saw who did this."

"I'm going to pack a bag and head to the airport."

"I'll have your ticket waiting."

"You're a good man, Darek. The best." She ended the call, and he turned around and looked at the little boy. He looked so small with the covers wrapped around him, and Darek knew he needed to get the kid somewhere he could get him some food and away from the chaos in the other room.

"Are you hungry, Noah? Thirsty?"

The little boy looked up at him, not saying a word. He looked to the door like he knew what was happening in the other room.

"Want to get out of here?" He knew the paramedics would want to look him over, and he had to follow protocol.

He nodded, his lips still pressed into a tight line.

"I'm going to take you out of here, okay? We'll get you checked over, and then I'll get you some breakfast while we wait for your auntie to come. It might take her a while. She's got to get in a big plane and fly over to get you." He thought if he kept talking it would distract the child from all of the chatter in the other room.

"There are a lot of people out there, and we don't want them to see us leave. So, what we're going to do is put this blanket around us and go really fast like a car, okay?"

Noah nodded. Darek lifted him up in his arms and wrapped the blanket around them. Then he covered Noah's face and hurried as fast as he could with the boy hanging on to him for dear life.

When they got out of the house, he held him in his lap while the EMTs checked him over.

In the distance, he saw Lizzy standing by one of the cars. She had someone on the phone, and she was chewing their ass out. He knew he should be in there working the case with her, but career or not, he couldn't let Raven or the boy down.

CHAPTER 22

CARTER

"Wake up, beauty, it's time to log into this thing again." Bay pushed the laptop across his lap and into Brandy's. She had dozed off next to him, and he had let the computer sleep while he looked at the messages and photographs on the old phone.

She moaned and stretched and gave Bay a big smile before typing in the password.

Carter didn't know how much more shit he could listen to between the two of them, but as long as they were getting along and Bay didn't want to try to kill her before he got his money, he wouldn't complain.

He had looked at so many naked photos that when he closed his eyes, all he saw were nipples.

Bay had returned the previous day, and the three had stayed in the living room the entire night, going through papers and photos. He had made sure Brandy dozed off before he did and was thankful for being a light sleeper. He didn't want her to tell Bay about their little deal, and so far, he'd managed to keep the other man in the dark. More money for the two of them.

"Anyone want coffee?" Carter asked, getting to his feet.

"I do," said Brandy. "Hold the poison and extra sugar?" She was so sweet to Bay, all she had to do was stick her finger in her mug.

"I like mine with a little cream," said Bay, not looking his way. "Thanks, Carter."

"Did you find anything to tell you who the woman is?" asked Brandy as Carter listened in from the kitchen.

Before Bay could respond, Carter's phone rang in his pocket. He pulled it out and frowned. He'd missed several calls. "What the hell is wrong with my phone?"

"The signal is weak in the house. You think that's bad? Justin had a scrambler to make it worse, but I turned it off. You still have to go out onto the porch."

"That's not at all convenient," mumbled Carter as he left the coffee brewing and walked outside, where the crisp morning air filled his lungs. The place was amazing. He wondered what it would be like to live there all the time, with the beautiful view and the sound of the river flowing in the distance. It was heaven on earth.

He dialed the number back and waited for Eddie to answer. "Carter?"

"Yes, of course, it's me. What's going on?"

"The brethren have been in a meeting all morning, that's what."

"What for? There wasn't a meeting on the books."

"There have been claims made against you. A woman is even claiming to be pregnant with your child!"

"What? Who?"

"Ava Lindsey, but she's not the only one. Keely Milton, she's come forward too. Apparently, the women got to talking and decided it was time the church pay for their silence."

"I'm working on that now."

"What?" screamed Eddie. "You knew about this, and you left town? Were you even working with the NYPD?"

Carter's gut was in knots. "Yes, I did, but the man I was supposed to interview hung himself in prison, and I've had to stay a little longer than expected."

"The hotel says you checked out two days ago."

Shit. "I'm staying with a friend. And I don't appreciate being treated like a child, Eddie."

"I've known you since you were a child, in case you've forgotten, so I know the difference. Skipping out on your responsibilities *is* childish! Fucking a member of the church who isn't your wife is childish. Should I go on?"

"Look, we'll just demand a paternity test and buy some time."

"We haven't let this get to your wife yet or the rest of the members, but the church is talking about replacing you with a fresh new face. Someone that everyone loves and who hasn't had their dick in half the congregation. They're talking about giving it to Todd. He's a good family man and more deserving, besides. While you've been diddling, he's been winning people's hearts and stepping up his game."

He had never heard Eddie be so angry toward him, not even when he'd fucked up in the past, but those times had been nothing like this.

"I'm sorry. I'm going to make it better! I'll call you later!" He hit the end button, not wanting to hear the disappointment in Eddie's tone again. He looked at his contacts and dialed Ava's number.

He couldn't believe after all they'd been through, after all he'd promised to do, she had gone behind his back and made this move.

She answered in a quiet voice. "Hello, Carter."

"How could you do this to me? I am here trying to get your fucking money, and you shit all over my life?"

"What about *my* life, Carter?"

"Are you really pregnant? Or is this just some elaborate scheme you two planned to come against me?"

Ava huffed. "You mean Keely? I saw that bitch leaving your office the other day. She admitted to fucking you."

"And so what? You and she got together and decided to turn me in? She meant nothing to me, and she came onto me first. You know that woman like my power, Ava. They see me as a challenge. I failed when it came to Keely, I'll admit that, but it's not because I don't love you. I would have done anything for you." He was so angry he could strangle her. And now he had to do damage control.

"Don't tell me that now, you piece of shit! If you wanted to show me you loved me, you should have given me the job I wanted. I applied for it before you idiots did away with the position, and that job should have been mine."

"And that's my fault? Why hurt me, Ava? If you claim to love me?"

"I *do* love you." She began to cry. "But it wasn't enough. You know, I put up with Adrian, mostly because she's so boring that I can't see you really enjoying her company, much less being infatuated or in love with her. But I can't take it when you don't stop at that. You just had to have another woman too. And you had to make it that slutty Keely Milton."

"Don't go through with this, Ava. Tell them that you lied, leave the church, and I'll line your pockets out of my own. I'll take care of you for life, angel."

"What about Keely? She'll never withdraw. She said you failed to send her some money she needed, and now she's being evicted."

Carter thought about the money he'd sent. He hadn't sent the other half he'd promised. He'd been so distracted by the trip and had left before she'd come back to see him. "Fuck," he whispered.

"Listen to you. You're not even the man I fell in love with anymore."

"I'm just angry and hurt, Ava. I love you, and now it's all gone to hell. And Keely is lying. I didn't owe her shit. She tried to take things further than a little slap and tickle and got upset when she was refused." He'd never admit to anything more.

"What about the child?"

Carter's face grew warm. "Are you really pregnant, Ava?" He hadn't really considered she could be telling the truth about that.

"Yes. It's why I was so upset that I'd been laid off. I hoped to keep it a secret for a while, at least until it was too late to abort it. I was afraid you'd make me."

Carter wasn't sure what he felt. He was going to be a father. He knew Ava hadn't been with any other men. She'd been too obsessed with him, and he kept her so well-bedded she didn't have time for anyone else in her life.

"Ruining me isn't going to help any of us." He should have cut her loose months ago. But part of him couldn't help but know that the baby was going to change his life for the better.

If he took the money and ran, he could take Ava with him and raise their child with her, or he could stay with the church and let it crumble. He didn't know what to do. He looked up and saw through the window where Bay and Brandy were laughing together. Bay's fake laugh was even creepier than his smile.

"I've got to go, Ava. I'm begging you not to say another word. I'll be home soon, and we'll deal with it then. I want to be in your life. Both of you."

"Fine. I won't do anything else until I hear back from you."

He breathed a sigh of relief and ended the call with another "I love you" he didn't really mean.

"Fuck, fuck, fuck," he said. "Stupid fucking bitches." He took a deep breath and walked into the house where Bay and Brandy were sipping coffee on the sofa.

"I see the coffee's made." Carter walked to the kitchen to get himself a cup.

Bay turned his head, giving him a narrowed stare. "Yeah, Brandy took care of it. So, what was that all about?"

"Just a few things at work that needed my approval."

"It sounded pretty serious," said Bay. "I thought you were screaming at one point. It was like music to my ears."

Brandy laughed.

"How long is this all going to take? Because I'd like to get back early if possible." Carter's whole world was falling apart, and he needed the fortune to make it all better. With him having his own fortune, one the church couldn't touch, he'd be fine no matter what they decided to do with him.

"We should be good to leave tomorrow. The store papers are all that's holding us up. I've got all of the other files sent to my email, so I can finish up from the comfort of home."

"Good," Carter said. "I'm ready to get back to the hotel."

Brandy gave him a cold stare like she couldn't wait either. "I should get down to the store. It's time to open up."

CHAPTER 23

DAREK

Darek stood across the room while Noah was being evaluated by children's services. They wanted to see if he was well enough to be questioned before they let anyone give him the third degree on a more in-depth level.

He hadn't talked much, just one-word requests, and he hadn't eaten anything, even though Darek sent out for donuts and chocolate milk.

Lizzy walked into the office, surprising Darek. She was supposed to be working on the scene, and he hoped that nothing bad had happened. "What's going on? Any good news?"

"No, they called me down here to check on you."

"Who is they?" He looked up to the desk, and the woman behind it averted her eyes. "Are you kidding? Why pull you away from the investigation?"

"It's okay," she said. "They've taken Honey's body to the medical examiners, and the forensics team is scouring the house for evidence, and then we'll have to lock it up once the blood is cleaned. The landlord is pissed off. I think Raven is going to be evicted, but the good news is, he can't make her move her things until the investigation is done."

"Wow, thanks."

"Yeah, I thought you might like to pass that along." She folded her arms and stared across at Noah. "When will she be here?"

"She should be here any minute." He looked at her and noticed her discomfort. "I'm sorry. I know this is horrible timing and puts you in an awkward position."

Lizzy turned and put her hand on his arm. "It's no worse than the last position you put me in with her, but I'm a big girl, and I can take it." She gave a shrug.

"Then, how come you look like you want to murder someone?"

She took a deep breath. "Did you have to call her 'baby'?"

Darek gave her a sideward look. He hadn't done that, had he? "I don't even remember saying it. If I did, it was a slip. I'm sorry."

"You know you can't leave with him, right?"

"What?"

"With Noah. You can't take him out of here, and they'll only let Raven take him if they think that she's going to be safe. They know there's a chance that Raven was the intended victim."

Darek narrowed his eyes. "How do they know that?"

"Because I told them. They needed to know. She's not this child's safest option, and neither are you."

"How could you do that? I promised to help Raven and Noah. I told this kid that his auntie was going to take him home with her." His temper flared, and his voice grew louder. "They can't just stick him anywhere."

"This is why they asked me to come down. They knew you'd act like this, and let me tell you, being angry here isn't going to do you any good either."

About that time, footsteps sounded behind him, and he turned to see Raven running across the lobby. "Darek!"

She saw Lizzy and stopped short of a hug, but she reached out and held his arm, the other hand over her mouth's twisted expression. "Where is he?" She looked over about that time and spotted Noah behind the glass. "He looks like his mother. Do I need to do anything for Honey? Make arrangements right away, or—dammit, I'm lost."

"It'll be okay, just calm down," he said, making damned sure not to call her "baby" or to be too touchy-feely, even though he wanted to pull her into his arms and hold her.

"When can I take Noah home? I know he's got to be worn out. Did he have any breakfast?"

"He wouldn't eat. I bought him some donuts and milk, and he didn't touch it."

Lizzy took a deep breath and pulled Darek aside. "You need to explain things to her. Do it now. Don't let it wait."

When she backed away, Raven had her arms crossed, and her eyes narrowed. "Is something wrong?" Her question was for Lizzy. Raven hadn't forgotten the way she'd been treated by the woman, and she probably had a good idea that Darek was back with her.

Lizzy gritted her teeth, and when her mouth opened, Darek stepped in front of her. "It's just that they probably won't let you take him."

"What? I've come all this way. I'm not leaving without Noah. I understand if I have to stay in town, but he's my family. I'm all he has left."

"And you're a danger to him," said Lizzy, raking her hand through her dark hair.

"I beg your pardon," said Raven.

"You've not only been questioned in a murder investigation, but now you could have been the intended victim. Child services are not going to let you take Noah under those conditions."

Darek gave her an apologetic look. "I'm going to do all I can."

Raven fell against him and sobbed. "Can I at least see him, talk to him?"

"Of course you can." He patted her on the back, and when his eyes met Lizzy's, she shook her head, walked over to the glass, and gave it a tap.

The counselor got up from talking to Noah and opened the door. After the two women whispered to one another, the woman shook her head and approached.

"You're Noah's aunt?"

"Yes, his mother is my cousin, and she's like a sister to me. We were raised together."

"I'm Marty Wallace. I've been assigned to Noah's case."

"When can I take him home with me?"

Marty frowned. "I'm afraid that might take some time. I'd like for Noah to stay with you eventually, but until we clear your situation with the police department and can determine that your lifestyle isn't a danger to the child's health and safety, then he'll stay in protective custody."

Raven nodded. "How's he doing? When can I see him?"

"He's doing good. I'm hoping he might open up a little, but so far, all I have determined is that he did, in fact, see his mother's body. Whether or not he saw the killer, that will be something for us to determine later. I don't want to pressure him so soon after the trauma."

"I just want to make sure that he's okay and hold him." Raven wiped her eyes, and Darek patted her on the back.

"Yes, ma'am, I understand. You can see him now." The woman walked on ahead as Raven dried her eyes.

She turned to Darek. "Will you wait until I'm done?"

Lizzy stepped forward. "Darek, I need you at work." She gave Raven an accusing glance. "We have a murder to solve."

Darek didn't know what to think, but he knew that Lizzy was right. He had to get on the case and get caught up. "She's right. I'm sorry. I texted you the hotel info, and if you go to the desk, they're all ready for you."

"Thank you." She fell into his arms and kissed his cheek before pulling away. "You're a good friend."

Darek looked up, and Lizzy was already down the hall. He let out a deep breath. "I'm sorry about her being here. I'll call and check on you. Take these." He passed her his car keys.

He hated to walk away, but he knew he had better catch up to Lizzy and make sure that she understood where he was coming from. And that she wouldn't leave him without a ride. Despite the way things ended, he cared about Raven and would always be her friend. His helping her was the decent thing to do.

He looked back as he got to the door and saw Raven pick up Noah and hug him tightly. That was all he had wanted to see, the two of them together.

He rushed out to the parking lot and caught up with Lizzy. "Wait up!"

"Why, did your *baby* need one last kiss?"

"It was a slip."

"Uh huh, and then she shows and you hug all over her?"

"I'm comforting her. Her cousin was just murdered, Lizzy."

"Yeah, because of the shit she's mixed up in. I told you from the start that she was involved, and you didn't listen. Instead, you kept fucking her, and now her cousin is dead, and a little boy is in foster care. And this could very well be the murder to set this damned case on its ear."

"What did you find?"

Lizzy handed him a small orange card, but when Darek looked at it closer, he realized it was no ordinary colored paper. It was covered in blood. The symbol on the card sent his pulse racing. The symbol was the most familiar zodiac to him. The same sign he'd worn on his arm all those years. "Sagittarius?"

CHAPTER 24

BAY

Bay turned the image and put it down next to the other. He had studied the damned photos for hours after they'd gotten back to the hotel room, and he finally put together enough pieces of the room behind the woman to piece together something that made sense to him. "Son of a bitch," he said with a smile.

"You found something?" asked Carter.

"Yes, I did. Look at this and tell me what you see." He backed away from the laptop and let Carter lean in.

The man got down closer and narrowed his eyes. "Is it supposed to be the worst photoshop I've ever seen?"

"It's the best I could do, but look closely. Do you see that it's a stack of clothes at least?"

"With a pair of shoes sitting on top?" He leaned in even closer. "Yeah, it's like a pair of black boots."

"Not just any boots. Police issue. I've seen those things enough to know."

"Couldn't they be military?"

"No, look at the little emblem and the stamp in the heel. It clearly reads PD. If I could just make out the letter in front of it. It's too grainy. But those are blue pants and a blue shirt. Police blue."

Bay waited for Carter to put two and two together.

"Wait, police blues? So that means the girl with the tits is a cop?"

"No, those boots are not small enough to be a woman's. Look at them in comparison with the rest of the background. They are huge."

"That could be a matter of perspective," said Carter. "Like how objects in mirrors are closer than they appear."

"Trust me, that chick with the little pussy doesn't wear those boots." Bay needed more photos, but Brandy hadn't let him look through the entire house, especially the safe room, where he had a feeling Justin would have hidden most of the dirt in his life.

"Darek. That fucking bastard. It's him." Carter paced the room, raking his hand through his hair. "He had Ken Sin killed."

Bay shook his head. "No, it's not Darek. But that doesn't mean that he doesn't know who it is, assuming that they are with the NYPD."

"What if this girl was just fucking some cop, and when he was gone, she fucked around online? How do we know she's Betty?"

Bay let out a grumble. He didn't see how Carter could memorize a bible verse, much less a sermon. "Because her phone number was consistent with the one that's messaging the rest of us. Haven't you ever gotten any messages?"

He shook his head. "No, but I changed my phone not long ago, number and all. I guess this killer couldn't get in touch through the office."

"Why did you get a new phone?"

"Obsessive weirdos wanting prayer. I didn't have time for it. I directed them to the staff, and they just kept calling me back. I'm not even sure how they got me. Maybe Ken Sin shared my fucking phone number. Who knows?" Carter walked back to the mirror. "I want to go out to eat tonight. I doubt this place has anything good on the menu, and I heard about a club that's thirty minutes from here I want to check out."

"How the fuck are you planning to get there?" Bay wasn't about to let him take his car.

Carter gave him a dirty look. "I thought you'd come with."

"No thanks. I'm going to finish up with those papers so she can sign them tomorrow and we can get back on the road. I'm sure this town has Uber."

"I guess I'll find out." He walked to the shower, and when he was inside, Bay looked out of the window and spotted the sporting goods store's sign in the distance. He looked at his watch and looked back at the bathroom where Carter had locked the door and turned on the shower.

Bay called through the door. "Hey, I'm going to go gas up and get me a drink. I'll be back in a few."

Carter stuck his head out. "Bring me a soda for when I get back later. And a candy bar or something."

Bay gave a nod. "Will do." He grabbed his keys, and after Carter went back to his shower, he headed out.

He drove down to Finch's Guns and Goods and pulled into the parking lot, hoping Brandy was right on time. He found her truck in the lot, and since it was such a nice day, he decided to wait outside.

He took out his phone and opened his text logs. "Hello, Betty," he mumbled as he typed.

There was no response. He decided to wait to tell the jerk he was onto them.

When Brandy walked out of the store, Bay sat on the tailgate of her truck with a big smile. She wasn't as happy to see him. "What are you doing here?" She looked over her shoulder. "Where's your friend?"

"I think he's going out to get laid one more time before going home to the wife."

She gave him an accusing look. "Is that what you're trying to do?"

Bay laughed. "Is that what you think I'm up to?"

"I don't know. I don't even know if I'm against the thought of it. I've been so lonely. Lately, I'm liable to do anything." She climbed up on the tailgate with him. "What did you come here for?"

"It's about the store. It seems that Justin wasn't as careful with his business as he was his home. And there's a little something you don't know that you should. I was one of two people who helped Justin remodel the store after his grandfather left it to him, and I also helped him build the second store."

"What's that got to do with the inheritance?" He saw her lip quiver and wondered if she were about to cry.

"Where the stores are concerned, it means that Justin never filed the correct papers, and the stores belong to me and my associate, or if I wanted to be a good friend and say I found proof that Justin did, in fact, file the correct papers, you'd still own eighty percent."

She gave a nervous laugh and shook her head. "You're just like your friend," she said. "And here I thought you were the sweet one."

"No, just the cute one. Although I wouldn't say Carter Hamilton is exactly a good man, either."

"What do you want, Bay? Do you want me to sleep with you? Do you want money?"

Bay let his gaze linger down her body. "The sex sounds good, but I'll pass. The money, however…"

"You two assholes came to pick me clean." She shook her head.

"Actually, I came to find out who killed my friends. But tell me more."

Her face fell, and Bay knew he had her. Her eyes and the panicked expression told it all.

"It's nothing."

"I know that Justin owed him some money." He wasn't going to show all of his cards.

Her back stiffened, her shoulders raising like ice water had been poured on her. "Yeah, again, it's nothing. He just came to remind me."

Bay smiled and met her eyes. "I have great admiration for someone who could lose everything dear to them and still come out on top."

"I didn't plan this to happen, Bay. I loved Corey. The rest just fell into place."

"And I might believe that if I were anyone else. But you see, Brandy, details are my business. I know there's always more to the story. People miss the small details. That's what I use to trip them up in court. I know how to twist the facts to get the outcome I want. That's why I can say I admire you. I think you do the same."

Brandy hopped down from the tailgate. "I've got to get back home."

"I read the report. You told the police that Justin's gun wasn't loaded, but that doesn't sound like the Justin I know. He would have never kept an unloaded gun in the house, especially one he used for self-defense."

"That's what happened," she said with a sharp tone. "I don't have to explain it to you. I cared about Justin, but he was just as crazy as the rest of you."

"And what do you know about my crazy? You think I'm a nice guy, remember?"

"I know plenty. Corey wasn't like the rest of you. He was good. He was sorry for what happened."

"And what was that?" Bay wanted her to say it.

She looked him in the eyes and shook her head. "I'm not telling you shit."

"Those secrets Corey told you, they put a target on you. They've taken the life of many others."

"Are you going to kill me, Mr. Collins? Take out all that's left of Corey?" She put her hand on her stomach.

"Now what good would you be to me dead?" He smiled like a snake, feeling just as dangerous. "I've got a proposition for you. And if you're smart, you'll take the deal."

Brandy's chin quivered. "I don't like ultimatums or men who abuse women."

"Look, I'm leaving first thing in the morning. And while I'm taking the preacher with me, I have a feeling it's not the last time that you'll hear from him."

"Corey wanted to take care of me. We were married in New Orleans in the hospital before he passed away. It's all legal. We would have told the others, but we decided to keep it private."

"Come on now. There's got to be more to that story. My friend didn't come here for the hell of it. He has something on you, something he's trying to use against you. I can make that go away, along with the property issue. I'll come by tomorrow, and we'll work it all out. You can sign the papers, and we'll get to the bottom of whatever problem you have."

"What's in it for you?" she asked with an accusing glare.

"We can work out a deal."

"Oh, of course, we can."

"I want the rest of the evidence. I want to go through Justin's house, all of it. Including the safe room." She looked away, her jaw twitching with anger.

"Fine. Come over, and we'll make it happen. I just want this shit over with. Can't trust any of you."

Bay stepped up where he was only a breath away from her. He looked down into her eyes, seeing the anger. "I can promise you this, Brandy. I'm a much better partner in crime than the preacher man." He had hoped that she would own up to her marriage not being legal, but neither one of them had the brains to come clean. If all went according to his plans, he'd get everything he came for.

CHAPTER 25

CARTER

Carter opened his eyes when someone knocked on the door of his hotel suite. As he rolled over, the warm body next to him stirred.

As it turned out, the club he'd found had a similar style as Taunt. Unfortunately, it was much harder to get rid of the hook up at the end of the night.

"Go away," he yelled.

Bay's voice called from the other side of the door. "It's me, asshole. Get ready. We leave in twenty."

He got to his feet, stretched, and then walked to the bathroom to take a piss. When he walked back into the room, the woman he'd picked up, who was a sexy redhead with no gag reflex, sat on the end of the bed where she'd left her dress which was wadded up and torn.

"Can I use your shower?" she asked. Her voice was scratchy, and her face was puffy.

Carter tried hard to remember her name but kept drawing a blank. "Sorry, I've got somewhere to be. You should leave." He knew he had to get rid of her fast. He didn't need her squatting in his room or trying to steal the towels.

He also didn't need to hear her complaints. He waited as she got her dress on, then stepped into her cheap heels. "It was fun, sweetheart."

"Fuck you, asshole," she said as she hit the door with her panties still in her hand.

He shut the door and shrugged. Then Bay opened the door. "Did you get rid of your skank?"

"She was sexy last night and gave a mean blowjob. It's probably better than what you did."

"I talked to Lila half of the night. She didn't shut up, so you're probably right. But we have to take these papers back to Brandy's house, and once I have her signature, we'll be good to go."

"What took so long on the property?"

"Justin is a sloppy businessman. The stores belong to me and Lane Simon."

Carter felt the sting of surprise. "You and Lane? I thought she got everything."

"It's just something that wasn't taken care of. I've made it right."

"Oh, so once this is done, she'll have full access to all of the money and properties?"

Bay grinned. "Full access. It's all hers."

"You don't still think she needs to die, do you?"

"You know, I think she's growing on me. If I had some insurance that she won't run her mouth, I'd reconsider."

Carter wasn't going to be the one to give him any insurance. He just needed them to get the signatures and get the hell back home. "I don't think she's going to say anything. She isn't worried about our pasts. She didn't let Corey's stop her from getting knocked up, and she was going to build a life with him."

"Well, let's go. I don't want to be all fucking day."

"I need a shower. I have to wash my junk and take a piss."

"Hope it doesn't burn, man. I hope you wrapped it up." Bay left to go back to his room, and Carter jumped in the shower. As he washed, he thought about the trouble waiting for him back home. It would be so easy to say goodbye to it all, to take Ava and the baby and move away, find a place that was just as nice as Justin's.

Carter's house was a palace with everything that money could buy, and he hadn't had to work for any of it. All he had to do was convince people the Lord loved them, and they would shower him with blessings. He had a gold toilet seat that someone had given him, and the floor in his shower was heated, so he didn't have to stand on the cold marble. It was nothing like the cheap plastic-coated fiberglass at his feet.

Justin's place was homey and comfortable, as well as a place the man could have been proud of. And that bitch was going to have it all to herself. Worse than that, she wasn't even going to use it. He wondered if he could make it a part of his deal. It would be worth it if he ever wanted to get away.

Bay pounded on the door minutes later as he dried off and pulled on his shorts. "I'm almost ready."

"You're worse than a fucking woman."

As Carter walked out of the bathroom, pulling on his shirt, Bay stood in the middle of the room holding his bags.

"Give me two seconds." He rushed over to grab his charger and then threw his toothbrush in the bag. He had his shoes on in no time and combed his wet hair back instead of drying it.

Two minutes later, they were on their way, and the best thing about the smaller town was the lack of heavy traffic to slow them down. They made it to the cabin in fifteen minutes, and the last five were spent going down Justin's long and winding road that still had Carter on edge.

When they pulled up at the house, Brandy was sitting on the porch with a glass of lemonade in her hand and staring at the trees.

Bay got out of the car and shut his door. "I take it you're ready to get down to business."

"Yeah, I think that's for the best," said Brandy. She turned to Carter and then back to Bay. "I've got that stuff you wanted."

Carter didn't understand what she was talking about, but it became increasingly obvious that she and Bay had talked about something.

"All of it, and I want to look around."

"So demanding," she said

Bay took a few steps closer to the porch. "You have no idea."

"Let's get this deal done." Brandy's tone sharpened.

"Sign these papers, and we'll talk about the deal later. I know you're anxious to have your property free and clear. Then you give me all the information I asked for, let me look around, and I'll take care of your problem."

Carter suddenly didn't know what to think. "What problem would that be?"

Bay walked up and handed Brandy a paper to sign. She did it without hesitation and smiled up at Bay after she signed the last one. "Now," she said, reaching toward the small table beside her. "Here's the rest of the photos, and I even threw in the phones. I don't need those for anything."

"Thanks, sweetheart." Bay smiled, not making a move to do shit.

"Well, I honored my part of the deal."

"You didn't let me look around. But that's okay. If I had a safe room full of weapons and money, I wouldn't let us in it either."

Her face fell. "How did you know about that? Justin said no one would ever know about it."

"I saw the blueprints."

"We had a deal," she said.

"I lied." Bay shrugged. "But then, so did you."

Carter was freaking out, and he was damned glad that Bay was his friend and not hers. "I told you she was crooked."

"You lied too, Carter. Too bad I already knew what was going on. The last time I talked to Justin, it was to thank me for the fake marriage license I had drawn up for you and Corey."

"You knew all along?" asked Carter, not believing his ears. "I guess I should have known Justin had someone else involved. It's cool, man. We'll put you in for an equal share."

Brandy reached behind her back and drew a gun, pointing it right at Carter's face. "If you think I'm going to let either of you take half of my money, you're sorely mistaken."

"I'm not going to take half of your money, Brandy." Bay stepped closer. "That's not the way I operate."

Carter knew exactly how Bay operated. He realized what he was up to. "You're going to take it all."

Bay smiled. "Damn straight."

Brandy kept the gun pointed at Carter as she turned to Bay. "You're nothing more to me than two more dead men."

Carter went to make a move for the car. Brandy turned back to him quickly and fired.

As Carter fell to the ground, another shot rang out. He looked up in time to see Brandy fall, and then Bay ran over to check on him. "How bad is it?" Carter asked, trembling and holding as much pressure on his wound as he could.

"She's a good shot," said Bay. "You should have fucking told me."

"I'm sorry. She's the only one who could get to the money. Do you realize what you've done?"

"Just what you said." He took the paper off the table from where Brandy had signed her name. "I'm taking it all. The stores, the money, the house. It's all mine now. But don't worry. I'll make a sizeable donation to your church in your memory."

Carter realized the papers had secured it all. He looked down and saw the blood as his pulse grew weaker. Surely, he wouldn't let another Zodiac die? He thought of his child. Of Adrian and Ava. He'd face them all just to have one more chance. "Save me, Bay."

Bay stood over him. "Sorry, brother. Only God can save you now."

To be continued...

The Zodiac story continues with Virgo

ABOUT THE AUTHOR

WL Knightly is a thriller/murder mystery co-writing pen name for USA Today Best Selling Authors Lexy Timms and Ali Parker.

When she's not writing, Lexy can be found dealing in Antique Jewelry and hanging out with her awesome hubby and three kids.

Ali is a CPA turned fiction writer who is married to her best friend and travels the US as a nomad. She spends her days writing, traversing the city and chasing her last kiddo in the house, a teenage quipper with too much time on his hands!

The two friends met years ago when they both started writing and publishing in various young adult genres and needed a critique partner. The rest is history…

Printed in Dunstable, United Kingdom